the

EXALTED
COMPANY OF
ROADSIDE
MARTYRS

WARREN CARIOU

the
EXALTED
COMPANY OF
ROADSIDE
MARTYRS

TWO NOVELLAS

COTEAU BOOKS

Edited by David Carpenter.

Cover shrine by Brenda Barry Byrne. Photo by Judy Boyer.
Cover and book design by Duncan Campbell.
Author photo by Glenn Cariou.
Printed and bound in Canada.

The publisher gratefully acknowledges the financial assistance of the Saskatchewan Arts Board, the Canada Council for the Arts, the Government of Canada through the Book Publishing Industry Development Program (BPIDP), and the City of Regina Arts Commission, for its publishing program.

Canadian Cataloguing in Publication Data

Cariou, Warren, 1966–
The exalted company of roadside martyrs
ISBN 1-55050-145-3

I. Title.

PS8555.A7366E9 1999   C813'.54   C99–920024–0
PR9199.3.C3445E9 1999

COTEAU BOOKS
401-2206 Dewdney Ave.
Regina, Saskatchewan
Canada   S4R 1H3

AVAILABLE IN THE US FROM
General Distribution Services
85 River Rock Drive, Suite 202
Buffalo, New York, USA 14207

In memory of my father, Ray Cariou,
who gave me stories.

Then I asked: does a firm perswasion
that a thing is so, make it so?

He replied. All poets believe that it does, &
in ages of imagination this firm perswasion
removed mountains; but many are not
capable of a firm perswasion of any thing.

William Blake

the

SHRINE
OF BADGER
KING

ONE

This afternoon I will drive Uncle Pious's old Moto Ski down the traplines and along the ditches to the shrine of Badger King, where, if I'm lucky, I'll find something that will lead to my salvation. Of course, I've learned not to count on being lucky. I may find nothing but snow in that accidental crèche, no clues to the whereabouts of Badger, no hints from the tongueless Virgin Mary. If my luck is particularly bad, the police might be waiting there for me, or someone less friendly than the police. But none of this can stop me. If I find nothing there today, I'll make the same desperate pilgrimage again tomorrow, and the next day, until I find some evidence of Badger and his minions. In case I fail, I'm writing this testament – every day, a little at a time – so the truth can live on without me.

It was five months ago when I first saw the shrine. Day sixteen of the election. Elvis and Vince and I were on a swing through the northern part of the riding, stopping for hand-shakes and acrid coffee at every gas station and greasy spoon on 496. We had spent the morning in Champlain, my old home town, parading from the campaign office to the nursing home to the brand new welfare building with a procession of relatives in tow. By the time we left, I was exhausted. Unfortunately, 496 was not the kind of road that encouraged napping, espe-cially with Elvis Sasakamoos at the wheel. I didn't even bother to close my eyes. There were more stutter bumps, hills, and hairpin curves per mile on that stretch of gravel than anywhere else on earth, and Elvis never slowed down for any of them. Sometimes I could swear he actually sped up for the rough spots, and then coasted on the straightaways to give the engine a rest. Surprisingly, the launching and slewing motions of the van didn't bother my sensitive stomach, perhaps because I'd travelled that road so many times in the early years. My intestines had paid their dues. Vince wasn't so lucky, but he had figured out long ago that complaining only made Elvis more reckless. All he could do was strap himself into the back seat, brace his legs against the back of Elvis's seat, and stare straight ahead at the horizon, like a dog in the back of a half-ton. His only solaces were Gravol and prayer.

Elvis's maniacal driving was actually one of the reasons I had made him my poll captain for the Dog River poll. He pro-vided the fastest ground transportation possible, and besides, anyone seen riding with him was automatically considered fearless. He was also a professional bootlegger, so whenever Vince and I were electioneering he could take the van and make deliveries of moonshine to strategic households. Up there, everclear was the best advertisement money could buy. But to my mind the most important thing about Elvis was his absolute, iron-clad dedication to me. In my third year of legal practise, before political life was even a gleam in my eye, I had defended his oldest son on a charge of attempted murder. The kid had been a bit too effective with his pocket knife during a brawl at a bush party. But since it was his first offence, I was able to get the charge reduced to aggravated assault. The kid got two years instead of ten, and I earned Elvis's eternal gratitude. This was a bigger accomplishment than I realized at the time, since every other Sasakamoos in the north later lined up against me, on the side of Badger King.

When we passed Hope Falls it was only 3:15, which meant we would still have time for a meal at Elvis's place before the rally. The only restaurant in Dog River was owned by a supporter of Iron Agnes Desrosiers, my main opponent, so we had decided to avoid the place – even though that meant eating Elvis's infamous caribou stew, which contained so many entrails that it looked more suitable for divination than consumption. I tried not to dwell on such a prospect. I stared out my window at the continuum of poplar trees beside the road. Their spring-green leaves were perfectly motionless until the van swept by and shivered them like sequins.

I thought about the stump speech I would deliver that evening in the school auditorium. There would be hecklers lying in wait near the back door, favour-seekers scuttling about like crustaceans, a handful of genuinely committed supporters, and a few sceptical, unattached constituents who were supposed to be so dazzled by my charm that they bought party memberships at the end of the evening. That was the best-case scenario. Dog River had been one of my strongholds in the previous two elections, but certain regrettable things had happened since my last visit there, and I didn't know what to expect anymore. Elvis had reassured me that I was still as popular as ever up there, but my recent failures had made me allergic to optimism. I didn't believe the people's memories could be so blessedly short, despite the statistics Vince was always trotting out to prove his theories of voter imbecility. The people might have told Elvis one thing, but they could very easily do something else on polling day.

As I was imagining the possible treacheries that the electorate could visit upon me, Elvis threw us into a sharp left turn, and the force pressed my forehead against the glass. In the apex of the corner I noticed, on the far side of the ditch, a miniature pyramid of boulders with a shiny piece of quartz perched on the top. A shrine. I had been trying to put them out of my mind, but it was impossible with so many reminders. There were at least twenty of them above Hope Falls, marking the most perilous corners, hills, and washouts on 496. Some were just rockpiles – cairns – near the roadside, or clusters of spindly crosses numbering the dead. I'm not sure how the tradition began, whether it was meant as a commemoration of the victims or simply a warning of the road's many hazards. The Church must have got ahold of it at some point, because the more recent sites were full-fledged sanctuaries, complete with seven-foot-tall statues of the Virgin Mary. Sometimes they decorated her with banners and plastic flowers, or enclosed her in a glass-walled hut to keep the birds away.

I remembered the times in my boyhood when I used to travel that same road with my Uncle Pious in his fish truck. He had a business for a few years hauling fish from the northern lakes down to Windfall. Driving was even more dangerous back then, when the road was two-thirds corduroy in summer and three-quarters ice in winter. His truck was a '47 Fargo with an oversized box and no suspension except the springs in the seat. Barrelling around those corners above Hope Falls with half a ton of frozen whitefish in the back never failed to raise my gorge. To keep my mind off the nausea, Uncle Pious used to tell me stories about the shrines we passed, and the people who had died there. *Rosa McKay, she roll Dizzy Baxter's truck when she's sixteen. Pregnant from Kenny Tootoosis, but. That's for the baby, that little cross there in the back.* After every story, he would reach under the seat for his crock of rye swish, take a long pull, and then pin the accelerator, as if eager to join the exalted company of roadside martyrs.

And now, according to the most reliable evidence, there was a new addition to that company. One fine midnight early in November, Badger King's legendary luck had apparently given out on him. He'd left a party in Hope Falls at about eleven-thirty and had managed to weave his way through forty miles of ice and snow before falling asleep at the wheel. At the end of one of the longest straightaways on 496, his old Plymouth Fury had plowed right into the trees. Nobody found him until the next afternoon, when the car was just a smouldering shell. That's how my sister had described it on the phone the next day. It had sounded to me, on the crackly long-distance line, like "smouldering hell."

God knows, I had wished him in hell enough times. But now, far from it, the accident scene had become holy ground. Not long after Christmas a member of my constituency executive had phoned to tell me that someone had propped a statue of the Virgin Mary against one of the trees up there. Before spring melt, the shrine was finished, and by all accounts it was one of the most elaborate ones in the north. I had tried not to worry about this, reasoning that it was to be expected: in the unwritten northern code, every road fatality requires a shrine. Still, I feared that Badger's shrine might become a rallying point for his supporters, or for the next generation of shit-disturbers who came along. Already there were superstitious rumours circulating about him in Dog River. The last thing I needed was a cult of Badgerism taking hold in my constituency.

Elvis was the only one I trusted up there when it came to information about Badger. He always had the inside scoop because his father, Narcisse, had been one of Badger's right-hand men. Usually Elvis gave me a Badger report within a few minutes of my arrival, but this time he seemed to have forgotten. I was not encouraged by this selective amnesia, which generally meant bad news, but I couldn't afford to go up to Dog River without knowing what was really happening there. Finally I had to bring up the topic myself.

"Much talk of Badger these days?" I asked.

Elvis was hunched over the instrument cluster like a deranged old lady. At first I thought he hadn't heard me, but then he pursed his lips, as if to kiss something slightly out of reach.

"Some," he said.

"I heard there's people who don't believe he's dead."

He nodded slowly, without breaking his focus on the upcoming corner. His face was always clenched, so he looked pissed off even when he wasn't – and now with his fresh Windfall brush cut he looked even more severe than usual.

"Angelle, she says he come around the house. And Marie

says. Nobody else says yet."

Angelle was Badger's last common-law wife. Marie was his adoptive mother.

"They should get some help," I said. "It's not healthy."

It was true that Badger had disappeared and subsequently resurrected himself more than once in his life. You couldn't blame people for hoping it might happen again. It was also true that the coroner had been unable to establish a positive I.D. on the body, since it was horribly burned and there were no dental records. But still, the consensus was that it couldn't have been anyone else. Badger was last seen driving away from that party at Hope Falls, and the next day a body was found in a burned-out Plymouth Fury that happened to have his licence plates. The evidence spoke for itself.

I looked back at Vince to see what he thought about all this. His pupils were Gravol-dilated, and his head was bobbing like one of those plastic tigers people used to put in their back windows.

"I think Vince here kind of misses him," I said.

He managed a snort. "Like a hole in the head."

"I know I do," I replied.

This was not exactly a joke, though I'm sure Vince assumed it was. As for Elvis, I suspected that he half believed me – or wanted to, at any rate. It would make his family life a great deal easier if I could make my peace with Badger. He had never mentioned the shrine to me, probably because his relatives were the ones who had built it.

Of course, after everything Badger had done to spoil my political fortunes, nobody could blame me for not mourning his death. When he was alive I had cursed him so many times that his name itself had become a profanity, synonymous with son of a bitch. Elvis knew this better than anyone. But somehow, now that Badger was gone, I couldn't justify holding that grudge beyond the grave. I thought I could be gracious – for Elvis's sake if nothing else. Besides, I really did miss Badger, in the same way you might miss a limb – a cancerous, gangrenous limb that's been amputated. Call it phantom enemy syndrome. You hate a man long enough, he comes to seem like a part of you.

There was something else too – a momentary perversion, a morbid whim that came upon me. Maybe I was seeking some verification of his death, or perhaps I wanted to celebrate the fact that I had outlived him. My original plan had been to pass by the shrine without so much as a comment, but now that the opportunity was upon me, I couldn't resist the chance to say goodbye.

"In fact, I miss him so much," I said, "I wouldn't mind stopping for a minute at this shrine I've heard so much about."

Elvis nodded curtly, as if a visit to the scene of my enemy's death had always been on the agenda. I thought I detected a slight increase in our already meteoric velocity.

"Twenty or so miles," he said.

Vince didn't say anything, but I could tell without even looking that his eyebrows would be jacked up to his hairline. He had never heard me utter one good word – or even a neutral word – about Badger King. I smiled, watching my wolfish reflection in the side window. I loved shocking him, even though it wasn't much of a challenge. Good old Vince. The Convincer, I use to call him, even though he objected to the criminal associations of the prefix. He was my media man, my own personal spin doctor, my guide to the manipulation of public opinion. But he was so gullible himself that I sometimes wondered about the value of his advice.

I was tempted to launch into an impromptu eulogy of Badger, just to see if Vince would believe me, but I knew Elvis wouldn't think it was funny, so I kept it to myself. We were silent for a while, probably each brooding on our own private memories of that renegade wildman who had made our lives unbearable the previous summer. In the next few miles, we passed four different statues of the Virgin, all of them facing the road with their arms held out like sleepwalkers. One was bleached bone-white by the sun. She reminded me of the plastic glow-in-the-dark St. Christopher my Uncle Pious used to have on his keychain.

I saw Badger's shrine from a long way off. The statue seemed to hang there at the end of the road like an apparition, shimmering in the dappled light that filtered through the trees. We drove into a hollow and the statue disappeared for a minute, only to spring up in front of us again just as we were coming to the corner. Elvis leaned heavily on the brakes and brought us to a shuddering halt. There was an uneasy silence in the van as we regarded the folksy diorama that marked the point of Badger's exit from this world. His car had sped straight past the curve sign and smashed a little crèche into the roadside poplars. It was perfect for the Virgin Mary. Unlike all the other statues, which stood in the barren road allowance like beatific scarecrows, this Virgin seemed to belong where she was, sheltered from the sun by a canopy of leaves. She was wearing the same powder-blue robe as all the others, and her hands were extended in the same gesture of welcome. The tree branches above her head were festooned with plastic gas-station-style banners that were fringed with multicoloured triangles.

I opened the door before Elvis or Vince could say anything to prevent me. As I walked around the front of the van I felt an insect crawling down my back, and I flailed at it involuntarily before I realized that it was only a meandering stream of sweat. I started to think this visit was not such a good idea, but it was too late to go back on my earlier bravado. The whole thing seemed preordained. I moved toward the shrine with a plodding reluctance, like a child called home for punishment.

I had expected Elvis and Vince to come along, but they stayed in the van, to leave me alone with the dead man's memory. Not that I wanted to remember. In fact, I decided to enact my own private ritual of forgetting. Since Badger wouldn't be thinking of me anymore, the least I could do was reciprocate.

From up close, the shrine reminded me of pictures I'd seen of Jim Morrison's grave. Like crazed rock fans, Badger's survivors had strewn pink fireweed flowers on the ground and carved elaborate messages in the tree trunks. *We love you Badger well see you in heven. You're ideas will live for ever in words & actions RVC & LML.* There was even a poem:

> *The Lord took Badger from this place*
> *He is mighty, full of grace*
> *And we all will see his face*
> *In our time and in our place.*

The first thing I thought when I read this was, *who* is mighty, full of grace? But I'd read enough tree-bark doggerel in my life to realize that the "he" was supposed to refer to the Lord. That generic elegy was probably carved beside every shrine from Hope Falls to the Elkhorn Muskeg.

Some of the trees had been scorched by the fire, and they exhibited their glistening wounds to the Virgin. Her face, turned slightly to one side, held a look of unfathomable sadness and compassion, as if she understood the suffering of the trees and every other agony of this world. There were strange red smudges on her bare feet, which I found on closer observation to be lipstick marks. And as if that wasn't enough, someone had tied a baby-blue lace garter to a branch direct-ly above her head. Not only was it tacky – the kind of thing the local studs like to hang from their rear-view mirrors – it was also the same colour as the Virgin's robe, which gave the impression that it had once adorned her leg. I'm no church-goer, but still I couldn't abide such blasphemy. I pulled the branch toward myself, untied the garter, and stashed it in my pocket.

Having made this contribution to the sanctity of Badger's shrine, I felt an unexpected sense of relief. I had been bracing myself to encounter something ominous in this crèche, but that possibility suddenly evaporated, and in its place there came a realization that Badger and I were finally free of each other. The best thing I could do now was to go forth and win the election. Nothing more could be done for Badger, short of tendering an apology to his departed soul, which was out of the question. He wouldn't have wanted me to pretend I didn't hate him.

I genuflected toward the Virgin and made a haphazard sign of the cross before turning back to the van. As I approached the road I looked over my shoulder for a last appraisal of the spectacle, to fix it in my memory. It seemed that all his reckless life he'd been hurtling toward this corner.

Elvis started the van, and I was about to climb in when I noticed the back of a flimsy pasteboard sign across the road, thirty yards north of the curve. It was blank on the side facing me, and that blankness suggested some interesting possibilities.

I didn't want to miss out on any of the local handiwork, so I jogged up the road for a peek. I don't know why I thought this was necessary. My visit to the shrine had already been more successful than I could have dreamed. All I had to do now was get back in the van and shut my eyes and savour my newly earned sense of redemption. But I was so brimming with benevolence that I felt almost invulnerable. I wanted to leave no stone unturned.

To this day I wonder if Elvis knew what was on the other side of that cardboard. He could have stopped me. Perhaps it was a test. As for myself, I was expecting a Magic Marker elegy, or maybe a pencil crayon sketch of the dear departed. I thought I might even scrawl in a verse of my own if there was room. I was already fumbling in my breast pocket for my pen when I saw what was on the sign. My first reaction was to clutch at my chest. It must have looked to Elvis and Vince like a coronary, but in truth I felt no pain at all. Only an instant collapse of my mental faculties. A raging sense of alarm left me temporarily unable to interpret this thing before me. I remember at first not reading the words at all, but only absorbing the shape of the letters. It was a professional sign. Professional, fire-engine red, with white lettering five inches high: BADGER KING: INDEPENDENT

An election sign.

I stood there for several heartbeats, gaping at the words as they wavered on the blood-coloured background. I was as mute and unmoving as the Virgin Mary across the road. Beyond the sign was the blocky shape of the van, its windshield a pattern of leafy reflections. I heard the radiator fan kick in, the engine climbing a brief arpeggio in response. I had to make an effort to overcome my bewilderment. When I finally succeeded, several explanations rushed into my vacant consciousness. The sign was a joke, or a protest, or an act of electoral mischief perpetrated by Badger's old cronies. But as sensible as these possibilities may have been, they were not much solace to me. I only knew one thing: the son of a bitch was bound and determined to ruin me, even from beyond the grave.

I hadn't entertained that thought for more than a second when I kicked wildly at the sign and snapped it off. I stomped on it, piercing my heels into Badger's name, mulching the paper into the weed-bound dirt. It felt so satisfying that I stood there on the shredded paper for a while, glaring down at my shoes as if Badger himself was beneath them.

Then I flew at the crèche. My shoes clattered in the gravel of the road, and I pulled down a cluster of swagging streamers as I made the turn toward the inner sanctum. I tackled the Virgin Mary. She was hollow plastic, and the sound of my chin hitting her breast resounded in her body. She went over backwards, and I hung on. Sky and branches and fluttering banners flew past the Virgin's wimple, and then we landed like a felled tree, bouncing twice.

The impact knocked the breath out of me. It seemed like I was wrestling with Badger King. I'd pinned him, but he had me in a bear-hug and wouldn't let go. I prayed for release, but at the same time I tightened my own grip until I thought my shoulders would dislocate. We were locked together like two fighting bucks, and I knew we would die there, entangled in each other's hatred.

Someone splashed moonshine in my face. I was lying in the back of the van, Elvis and Vince dangling above me like absurd puppets. I could tell they had been arguing about something and had only stopped when they saw I was awake. I had never seen their faces from so close, and in my delirium I was fascinated by the corrugated skin of Elvis's forehead. It was lined with ruts like a springtime grid road.

"Minister?" Vince said. He always called me that, and I hated it. "You all right, Sir?"

I concentrated on breathing, trying to move the air without disturbing the band of pain along the edge of my ribs. "I'll never escape that bastard," I said. "Will I?"

Instead of answering, Elvis held the bottle up to my lips.

TWO

I should have known that Badger was not the type to run for public office. He was a shit-disturber, not a politician. He'd always had a problem with authority, which is not surprising when you consider his upbringing. His first few years in Champlain, he had free reign of the place because his father was the only cop in town. His parents knew he was a hellion, but they had long since given up their attempts to control him. They chose instead to cover up his transgressions whenever they could, in the name of respectability. At the same time, he was trying his damnedest to overcome the stigma of being the cop's son. You had to be spectacularly delinquent to make up for parentage like that, but Badger was certainly successful. There was nothing to stop him from doing whatever the hell he pleased, so he did. He became a tire-slasher, a freelance arsonist, a torturer of neighbourhood cats. One time when he was fifteen, he broke into the school and crapped on the principal's desk. I heard him bragging about it in the pool hall the next day, but none of the authorities ever questioned him. Not long after that, he dropped out of school altogether and started leading a band of adolescent thieves who made a pastime out of stealing everything from chocolate bars to heavy equipment. Half the gang got sent to reform school after they stole the municipal backhoe and used it to pry the roof halfway off the liquor store. My little brother was one of the idiots who got caught in there the next morning, too drunk to climb back out. Everyone knew Badger had been there too, but he was never charged.

Nobody called him Badger then, of course. His real name was Francis Cameron. He must have decided some time during his first disappearance that he would never make it as a renegade with a waspy name like that. It didn't matter that he named himself after an animal that doesn't even live in the north. What counted was the way people treated him when they learned about his name, as if they expected nothing but belligerence and tribal wisdom to emanate from his mouth. He was particularly skillful at playing this role when he had an audience of news reporters, who loved to think of him as a noble savage. They probably assumed he was a treaty Indian, after seeing his braids and buckskin, and after hearing all that talk about "his" people. But in fact he was a halfbreed, just like me. His old man was as white as they come, and his mother was a non-status Cree. It always amazed me that those same reporters assumed I must be white, just because I wore suits and drove a new car. Maybe it's like Vince used to say, perception is reality. Whatever the people think you are, that's what you become.

Most of us thought Francis was a pain in the ass. Him and Fucksakes Merasty used to hang out all day in the pool hall and pick fights, even though they hardly ever won. I was three years older than Francis, and in the year before I left for university I must have thrashed him a dozen times. He was the mouthiest little bastard in town. His all-purpose answer to any question was, What's it to you? – a phrase he repeated so often that he pronounced it as one word. Whatsittoya. He had a way of squinting and lifting his chin at you while he spoke. I remember Fucksakes used to lean against the jukebox and whine encouragement, but he always snuck away to the bathroom just in time. Francis never knew when enough was enough. The only way to shut him up was to drag him out the back door and punch him in the face once or twice until he fell down. It was always easy to hit that bulbous, cartoonish head.

One thing I will say for him: he never told his old man that I was the one who had been giving him the black eyes. If he had, it could have meant endless misery for me, since Constable Cameron was notorious for destroying anyone who crossed him. With a few trumped-up charges, he could have ended my political career before it even began. But maybe the

Constable was too distraught to concentrate on revenge that summer, or maybe I wasn't very high on his list. On the long weekend in May, his wife had taken off to Vegas with one of the Uranium miners from Saskatoon. The whole town knew about it. People were laying bets on whether or not she would come back. By the middle of June, the Constable requested a transfer, and he was gone to the Northwest Territories before the summer was up.

Like an idiot, Francis refused to go along. I think he was the only kid in Champlain who wouldn't have given his right arm to get out of there, even if it meant living in some other one-horse town further north. I guess he didn't know what Champlain was like for the rest of us, since he'd never had to worry about the law. Or maybe he wanted to wait around for his chance to settle scores with everyone who had drubbed him. For whatever reason, he ran away and lived in a trapper's cabin that fall, until he turned sixteen and his father couldn't force him to move away. Then he came back into town and set up shop in the pool hall, selling reefers and moonshine and whatever the neighbourhood kids could steal for him. Marie King, a widow with grown-up children, felt sorry for Francis and let him live at her house. She never had a clue what he was up to. For all the time he lived with her, she thought he was still going to school.

After I left for university, I didn't see Francis much, which was fine with me. I only came back to Champlain a couple of times each term, and in the summers I worked in the city. Occasionally when I was home I saw him selling his wares at a bush party or at the pool hall, but we never exchanged more than a few words. He didn't pester me any more. I wouldn't say that he forgave me for the bruises and the humiliation I had given him over the years, but he had learned to stop provoking me. He seemed to be maturing, at least a little, and I suppose I was too. If our relations had continued that way, it's possible that our conflict would have dissolved into mutual indifference, and eventually into complete oblivion, so that by now I might not even recognize the name of Francis Cameron. But on Remembrance Day weekend, 1973, that gradual disconnection of our lives was suddenly reversed. Our meeting then was what galvanized our animosity, what perhaps made everything else inevitable.

Back then they used to give us a long weekend for Remembrance Day, and I had come back from law school to help Uncle Pious with the whitefish harvest, because the first week after freeze-up was always his busiest time.

The temperature change never fails to send the whitefish into a frenzy of activity, and they jam themselves like cordwood into the nets. The only trick is, to get at them you have to walk out on that cardboard-thin ice, or chop through it with an axe from the front of your boat. Neither of these activities was considered safe for a man of Uncle Pious's age. He was over seventy, and his eyesight was so bad he couldn't tell an elk from a palomino anymore. He had shot Lars Parison's favourite horse the previous fall, and hadn't noticed his mistake until he was half finished gutting the animal, when he grabbed one of the hooves and realized something wasn't right. Since then, my parents had been trying to harangue him into retirement. They thought they'd better stop him soon, before he wandered off the edge of the ice into open water, or leaned too far out of his boat and dropped over the side like a lost fish. Of course, their suggestions only fuelled his determination to keep at it, come hell or high blood pressure. He even refused to let anyone help him – except me, but then I was a recognized handicap. My incompetence in all matters mechanical had long been a source of shame to my family.

I remember I got up early on Saturday morning and blundered around the house through the viscous haze of an Extra Old Stock hangover. I'd been up until four drinking with my brothers and their friends. My oldest brother Leon had said he would give me a ride up to Uncle Pious's cabin, but when I knocked on his bedroom door he told me to go to hell. Dad had already taken the truck out to Jimmy's Garage on 496, where he had a job for the month fixing snowmobiles. Mom was over at Josephine's place doing laundry. I didn't dare phone Uncle Pious to come over and get me, since I knew he would be safer going out alone in his boat than driving half-blind on the Keskemay road.

At nine I heard a female voice coming from Leon's room, so I realized it was pointless to wait for him. This meant I would have to walk the three miles out to Jimmy's and ask Dad for the truck. Leon's Cordoba was parked in the back yard, but I didn't dare take it without permission. I jogged down the frozen dirt road with my hands in the front pockets of my jeans. There was only a skiff of snow on the ground, but already the air was cold like gasoline. The sun had risen from behind the hockey rink, and through the high clouds it shed just enough light to reveal the true ramshackle character of the houses on our block. Coulloniere's place was painted lime green, Bileau's was fuscia, and ours was ultramarine, yet somehow all of them still looked drab and dusty, as barren as the poplars that crowded the edge of the lake. It had taken me three years of city life to understand the true sadness of that scene. To this day, fluorescence depresses me.

I turned north on main street, past J&J Grocery, where three frosty cars were wedged up against the boardwalk. I thought I might stop in at the café for some coffee and warm air, but before I reached it I noticed a burgundy Chev half-ton idling down the street toward me. It wasn't more than a year old, but already the paint was badly scraped on the driver's side. Behind the cab was a huge CB antenna the length of a fishing rod, with a ragged fox tail tied onto the end. The windshield was mirror-tinted, so I couldn't see inside, but still I knew who was driving. My brothers had told me all about Francis's new purchase. He was probably just limping back to Marie King's place after last night's party.

I had no interest in renewing my acquaintance with Francis, but I didn't want to ignore him either, because I knew that might make him try all the harder to piss me off. Besides, from what I had heard, he was no longer just a teenage annoyance anymore. My brothers talked about him differently from the way they used to. They still shook their heads at the crazy things he did, but they were careful not to call him a shithead or a goof or anything else that might be considered an insult. I could see the prudence of this. For one thing, Francis was the main connection for drugs in town, and anyone who crossed him would be left off the delivery route. It was also worth considering that Francis had grown-up into a sizeable man, a man with a recently-earned reputation for punching people's lights out in the hotel bar. It seemed that he had finally learned to fight, after all those years of practice.

I'm a big man myself, and I wasn't about to avoid Francis just because he'd landed a few punches on some drunken idiot in the Champlain bar. But still, I was past the age where I went looking for trouble. As the truck approached me, I gave Francis a brief nod and then looked away, as if to concentrate on charting my course through the uncertain territory of main street. Unfortunately, this was all the encouragement he needed. When the truck was almost past the grocery store, it swung around and nosed smoothly toward me. One front tire connected with the boardwalk, and the vehicle rocked back and forth, so I could hear the fuel slopping in the tank. Francis was a vague blurry presence behind the slippery reflections on the windshield. He kept the truck running and sat there for a few seconds before he rolled down his window and leaned an arm out on the side mirror.

"Where you goin, city boy?" he said. He focused on the back of his hand, as if speaking to a bank teller during a robbery. His eyes were so bloodshot they looked like bullet wounds.

"Pool hall," I said, though we both knew it didn't open until noon.

"Ch!" He lifted his chin at me, just like old times, except it didn't make me want to hit him anymore. It was not so much defiant as ridiculous. I felt almost sorry for Francis, despite his new reputation for toughness. He would probably never know how much of a joke he really was.

"Looks like business is good," I said, gesturing toward the truck.

He laughed. "You think I'll need you some day. Big lawyer. No chance."

"Tell you what," I said. "Give me a ride out to Pious Janvier's place, and I'll owe you some free advice."

I didn't have time to think about what I might be getting myself into. He gunned the engine, ran a hand through his long greasy hair, smoothed his flaring sideburns.

"Get in. But I'll never need it."

The truck smelled like a fish-smoking shack. In a matter

of months, he had managed to eradicate the factory aroma of a brand-new vehicle and replace it with his own special blend of herbs and spices. Most of them illegal. An eagle-feather roach clip swayed from the rear-view mirror, along with an acorn-shaped air freshener that only served to emphasize the odour of smoke. The seat was covered by a red wool blanket with dozens of tiny burns in it. This was a bona fide reefer wagon, stuffed to the visors, no doubt, with psychoactive substances. Not that I hadn't tried them myself in my day, but now I was worried about getting a criminal record and not being allowed to practise law. I had to trust that Francis was still as good at avoiding the heat as he used to be.

We backed out onto the road, the tires thumping in the frozen ruts and footprints. Francis wrenched the column shifter toward first gear but missed.

"Grind me a pound of that," I said.

He didn't think it was funny. He unleashed a seething horde of curses, then double-clutched and tried again. It worked this time. We jumped forward, the back end fishtailing, rocks hammering against the undercarriage. At the end of main street, where the cenotaph loomed, Francis cranked the wheel and we swooped to the right and up First Avenue without even slowing down. He had turned the wrong way, but I assumed he had his reasons so I didn't say anything. Uncle Pious lived on the far side of Champlain Lake, about twenty miles down the old road, and you had to go two miles south of town before reaching the turnoff. Francis was heading north, toward the lake itself. First Avenue was a flurry of aluminum trailers, unpainted sheds, rusty cars, and drydocked wooden scows interspersed with perfect conical spruce trees, some of them already sporting strings of Christmas lights.

"He's on the north side," I said. "Past Keskemay."

"I know."

We didn't have a radio station up there then, and Francis's CB was switched off, so all we could listen to was the snarl of the engine and the syncopated rhythm of the tires in the ruts. I opened the glove compartment and looked through it, trying to appear nonchalant about his driving. I found the owner's manual, a heavy pipe wrench, a satchel of Drum tobacco, a pack of rolling papers, three plastic lighters, and a handful of rifle shells.

"Lookin for something?" Francis asked.

"Just looking. Nice wrench you got there."

I pushed the compartment shut and leaned back in my seat. There was a vague smile on Francis's face, but he didn't say anything. He slowed down a little, then reached up to the instrument panel with his left hand and pulled out the speedometer. It hung there by its wires like a half-disconnected eye.

"Maybe this is what you want," he said, pulling three fat plastic bags out of the cavity and tossing them one at a time onto my lap. Each contained at least a dozen smaller bags, all neatly labelled. There must have been ten or twelve ounces in total – enough to keep the whole town stoned for more than a week. Which was, I suppose, Francis's ultimate goal. Now I understood why he was trying to be friendly. Just doing business.

"The smaller one – there – that's the best I ever had. Mexican Red Hair. Better'n Sensimillian even."

I opened it and sniffed. The whole experience of high school came back to me. For a moment it was like I had never left Champlain at all.

"Nice," I said. "Unfortunately I'm broke. But I'll keep you in mind when my ship comes in."

He exhaled loudly. "You do that."

We had been circling the deserted gymkhana grounds on the outskirts of town while Francis gave me his sales pitch, and now he turned back north toward the lake. As we came up to the church, he eased off on the throttle and pulled into the parking lot beside the rectory, overlooking the shoreline. He shifted into neutral and kept the engine humming at high revs while he stuffed his precious bags back into the instrument panel and replaced the dangling speedometer. When he was finished, we stayed there for a long time, staring out across the newly formed ice which was laid like Saran Wrap over the water.

I still don't know if the idea came to him at that moment or if he had been planning it all along. I remember suddenly realizing, by the demented grin on his face, that he was considering something crazy. There was an unofficial contest every year in Champlain, and the winner got free drinks for a week at the hotel bar. To win, all you had to do was be the first one to drive across the lake.

"How about a shortcut to your Uncle's place?" he said, glancing over at me with the same taunting look that used to come into his eyes when he was getting himself into trouble in the pool hall. He still thrived on danger and stupidity.

"That ice has only been in two days," I said.

He gunned the engine and slid the shifter into first.

"Like walking on water," he said. "You're my witness."

Then he dumped the clutch and we spun out of the churchyard, spraying stones against the rectory and Father Archambault's old Mercury. He cranked around the corner toward the boat launch, then let off the gas momentarily. I still didn't believe he would do it. On the other side of the lake, Uncle Pious would be in the front of his boat, chopping through that same ice to get to his nets. There couldn't have been more than an inch of it.

But when we turned onto the sandy passageway that served as a boat launch in the summer, Francis matted the accelerator. His eyes were fixed on the frosty rim of the far shore, three miles away. The trees beside us disappeared, and there was a moment of pure openness on the beach before we got to the ice. I grabbed for the doorhandle but was too late.

When the front wheels hit, there was a thunderbolt below us. I could feel the heave of the ice, its elasticity gathering us in like a trampoline. Cracks travelled out at a hundred times our speed, splaying themselves in all directions, ricocheting off the shore and bouncing back out. The rear wheels spun furiously, whining against the ice. But we didn't go through. We were still on top. That was all I needed to know. I opened the door and flung myself, like a diver, onto the splintering surface.

I landed so hard I thought I would punch my own hole in the ice. But it held, and I kept sliding beside the truck for a long time, first on my right side and then over on my back. Each new crack was like an explosion that seemed to echo, causing smaller detonations further out. The sky above me rotated slowly, wheeling the sun around in loops. Finally I stopped. I rolled over onto my stomach to look back at the truck. It was still going, the open door flailing, the tires still worrying the ice, that crazy fox tail whipping along behind like a battle standard. A crack shot out from the truck like an arrow, directly toward me. As it passed beneath me, it seemed like I too was split. I sprawled out my arms like a crucifix and waited for the lake to swallow me. The ice burned on my cheek. I could see through it and down to the brownish fronds and furry water mosses that carpeted the bottom.

I said a prayer for myself, and I pronounced an elaborate curse upon the soul of Francis Cameron. Then I started to shimmy, along the crack that had split me, back toward

Champlain. A shallow trail of water was seeping up where we had driven, so I had to choose another way. I aimed for Johnny Weasel's cabin, just off the point. I had no gloves, so I had to put my hands in my pockets and go on elbows and knees. I measured my progress against the lake bottom, crawling from hibernating fern to curled-up lily pad to sunken log. The ice sagged beneath me, and moaned and squealed, but it didn't fracture. There was someone on shore, waving a red hat and yelling to me. I looked back for the truck but couldn't see it.

The guy on shore tested the ice gingerly for a few seconds, and then started coming out to me. I kept crawling. In the shallower water, minnows and water beetles hurried out of their hiding places to escape me. My rescuer was standing up, striding toward me without even looking down. His eyes were on the far shore. When he was thirty feet away he yelled out to me.

"He made it! The crazy son of a bitch made it!"

I knew the voice. It was Fucksakes Merasty. He whooped and jumped up off the ice to kick his heels in mid-air. When he landed, one foot went through. I flattened myself again, hugging the ice as the cracks flew past me. Then I started toward him, squirming like a snake across the surface. I could feel the waves passing through it, could see the water welling up out of the hole and dropping back down like blood from a wound. He had managed to pull himself back onto the ice and was reaching toward me. I grabbed his hand and started tugging him away from the hole. When we were almost to shore I leaned over him to ask if he was okay. That was when he recognized me.

"You!" he said. "Why the fuck didn't he take me?"

Until that moment I had just been praying to make it to shore alive, but when I heard the scorn in his voice I realized that this was not the end of my troubles. What he meant was that *he* wouldn't have bailed out. That was easy to say when you could see the truck safe on the other side, but I knew it was what everyone else in town would say too. If Francis had gone through the ice, I would have been congratulated for escaping, but since he had made it across, I would become the village scapegoat. For every bit of glory that Francis received in the hotel bar that evening, an equal amount of derision would fall upon me. And I knew Fucksakes would be leading the parade, telling everyone how he had found me crawling homeward while Francis careened across the water.

You might think I would no longer care what that bunch of backwoods hicks thought about me. But I did. I cared desperately – so much that I thought it was perfectly reasonable to kick Fucksakes Merasty in the stomach as hard as I could. His body seemed to curl around my foot, and a single barking sound came out of him before he collapsed on the ice.

"You keep your fucking mouth shut," I said. "There's a hell of a lot more where that came from."

He didn't answer. I watched him squirming there for a while, and then I turned back toward town. There was a path through the bush behind Johnny's place which I hadn't taken since I was a kid, when we used to come out to the point every spring to watch the suckers and whitefish spawning. I trudged along that childhood trail, but there was no room in my mind for reminiscences. The bare trees provided little shelter from the wind, and soon I was up on the road, where I was completely exposed to the elements once again. I realized how dangerously cold I was. But I didn't stop at the church, or at the café, or even at my own house. I kept walking, doubled up against the wind, my hands jammed down into my jacket pockets. I climbed the hill at the far end of town until I reached the RCMP detachment, which was perched up there like a sentry post. When I was younger I had been terrified of the place, but now I thought of it as a symbol of justice and truth and all the other virtues I had learned about in law school.

There was no party for Francis that night, even though he had won the contest. When he showed up at the bar to collect the first instalment of his prize, the Constable was waiting there for him. And somehow the Constable knew exactly where to look for the stash of illegal substances.

It took Marie King four days to came up with enough money for Francis's bail, and by that time my brother Leon had driven across the lake and had been declared the victor. Francis tried to take the credit anyway, but nobody believed him. Fucksakes Merasty kept his mouth shut for once, and I was already back in Saskatoon. Since there were no witnesses, his miraculous drive might not have happened at all.

THREE

Francis was charged with possession for the purpose of trafficking, and he appeared before a hardass judge who sent him off to the Prince Albert Pen for two years. He served half his time there, and then he was paroled in Regina for another year. After that, he simply disappeared. To this day, no one knows where he went for those twelve years. Or at least no one will tell *me*. I tried to track him down for a while, through some of my contacts in law enforcement and corrections, but I came up with no reliable evidence. After two or three years of occasional inquiries, I finally gave up and decided to live my life as if Francis Cameron was gone for good. But I'll admit that not knowing his whereabouts continued to make me nervous. I had begun to practise law in Windfall by this time, and I was newly married, and was starting to consider a career in public office. I had been lucky, and my good fortune made me feel vulnerable.

There were plenty of rumours about Francis's disappearance, of course, especially up in Champlain. Everyone had expected him to come back there and resume his former life, and when that didn't happen, people started fabricating all kinds of stories. A lot of them believed he was dead. Some thought he had gotten himself mixed up with the Mafia, or that he had crossed the wrong people in jail. There was another story that he had come back to Champlain, overdosed on LSD, and tried to walk on the waters of Lake Kichitanga. Other people thought he was still alive, and that he had joined a gang of desperado bikers who roamed the continent robbing banks and selling cocaine. Two possible sightings of him were reported: one in a grocery store in Edmonton, the other at a motorcycle rally in Grand Falls, North Dakota. Old Marie King never lost faith that Francis was going to return. The story in Champlain was that she wrote letters to him, once a week, and kept them in a trunk at the foot of her bed, awaiting the day of his arrival. Maybe she knew something the rest of us didn't.

Things got worse in Champlain during the years that he was gone, though his absence had nothing to do with this. The poverty had always been terrible, but now the people began to lose all hope. Tuberculosis started making a comeback. The trappers lost their markets because of fur embargoes in Europe. The fish stocks in the big lakes became so depleted that commercial fishing was no longer viable. The old ways of life were disappearing, but there was nothing new to replace them.

Down in Windfall they had the pulp mill to generate economic activity, but in the northern areas there was nothing for people to do except gamble and drink and wait for the next government cheque. That was the main reason I finally decided to run for elected office: I wanted to do something for my homeland, to make a difference, so my people could learn to hope again.

I think the decline in conditions up north was also part of the reason that the stories about Francis Cameron persisted. He came to symbolize a time when the north was a colourful place rather than a landscape of unrelenting despair. People talked about him with a certain wistfulness, forgetting entirely that they had considered him either an annoyance or a terror when he lived there. To them, he was the cop's son who went bad, the guy who had pried the roof off the liquor store, the peddler of sundry intoxicants. They admired his pluck, his audacity. Listening to their stories, you would have thought he was a Robin Hood or a Falstaff, a merry rogue who really meant no harm and who spiced up life in an otherwise dull town. And Francis was all the more interesting because he had disappeared so mysteriously, which meant that he was neither quite dead nor quite alive – and that he might reappear at any time. I think they wanted him to return. And maybe he sensed this, because finally he did.

He didn't go to Champlain though; he came to me. After twelve years of absence, he tracked me down in my Regina office and barged in to declare his intentions. I didn't quite understand him at the time, but in later years, when I saw his plans unfolding, it all became abundantly clear.

I was still a backbencher then, so my office was in the basement of the legislature along with all the other government MLAS. It was a sweltering day in June, and the house was still in session because we were battling with the socialists over the merits of privatization. The thrill of our second election win the previous year was already beginning to fade, now that we were faced with a barrage of filibusters, petitions, and incessant bell-ringing. There were a lot of protestors in the building at the time, which is probably how Francis managed to waltz right past the security guards without arousing suspicion. Still, it was a travesty, since he looked like a madman. We politicians spend millions of dollars protecting the public from themselves, yet when it comes to our own security, we hire doddering World War II veterans and arm them with walkie-talkies. It takes an unpleasant surprise to change our priorities.

I remember I was sitting at my desk reading the *Leader-Post* when the door flew open and a huge, greasy lunatic came storming in. He slammed the door behind himself, shot home the deadbolt, and then grabbed one of my wooden chairs and jammed it under the doorhandle. There was something in his left hand which I realized, when he turned to face me, was a knife. At that moment I recognized him.

"Francis, you ugly fuck," I said.

If I had taken some time to consider the situation before speaking, I probably wouldn't have said that, but my first reaction to his presence was pure contempt, and I was too surprised to be frightened. In any case, it seemed to disarm him momentarily. He flinched when I said it, and something of his old hangdog disposition reappeared. It was the look of sudden incredulity that used to flash on his face just before my fist connected with his jaw. But this time he recovered quickly. He turned the knife in his hand, and the fluorescent lights gleamed along its length. It was a hunting knife, with a home-made deer-antler handle and a notch on the base of the blade for bloodletting. His belly hung out over his jeans like a garbage bag full of water. His hairline had receded about three inches, but still he had managed to grow two braided ropes of brown hair that hung stiffly down his shirtfront.

"Mister Kenny Janvier," he said, performing a mock curtsy, waving the blade with a flourish. Then he stepped back, grabbed his crotch with his free hand, and hoisted it up as far as his filthy jeans would allow. "Honourable Member!"

I tried to laugh, but by this time the seriousness of my predicament was becoming clear. I might have been able to take him in a fistfight, despite my years of sedentariness, but I knew I couldn't defend myself against that blade. And it was obvious that he wasn't bluffing. He had every reason in the world to carve me up. I had ratted on him. In his criminal world, ratting was the only real crime, and it deserved the cruelest punishment.

I started to panic a little at that thought, and in order to disguise my uneasiness, I resorted to belligerence.

"You better put the toy away," I said. "Your daddy won't get you off the hook this time."

He lifted his chin at me. "We'll see who's on the hook," he said, and he waved the tip of the blade at me again, making a sideways figure-eight, an infinity sign. I thought he might lunge at me right then, but instead he pulled up another chair, wedged himself down into it, and swung his feet up onto the desk. He stunk of some infernal mixture I had never encountered before: bodily excretions left to ferment and fester for so long that they had mutated into something completely alien. I thought he might be drunk, but it was impossible to tell from the odour. More likely it was LSD, or some kind of flashback. But no matter what else might have been affecting his behavior, he was also certifiably insane. I could see that in the unblinking luminosity of his eyes and in the way the knife kept twitching, sometimes tapping against the arm of the chair.

There was an emergency alarm button under my desk which I could have hit with my knee, but I knew it would only summon those gouty old codgers who shuffled around the building all day, and I was sure Francis would make short work of them. I had to find some way of appeasing him.

"Drink?" I asked, and he smiled broadly, displaying the

mossy stumps of his incisors. The knife was utterly still for a moment. I reached, slowly, for my file cabinet and pulled out a twenty-six of Crown Royal and two tumblers, which I filled. I slid one across the desk toward his dusty bootsoles. He lifted his feet off the desk and eased them to the floor, then reached over his belly for the glass. He took it and leaned back, inhaling the bouquet like some kind of connoisseur.

"So," I said. "What brings you?"

He seemed surprised at this, as if his intentions were perfectly obvious. I expected him to say "revenge," but he didn't. He took a short breath to speak and then hesitated for a moment, looking up at the ceiling for inspiration. He saw something there, some luminous vision of the future or the past that seemed to animate his thick and dogged features.

"I want to live on," he said, and gazed at me with slovenly beatitude. The earnestness in that bovine face was somehow far more frightening than the quivering knife in his hand.

"Live on what?" I asked. "Welfare?"

He smirked, and the glow in his eyes seemed to falter for a second.

"Just live on. Same as you."

He raised his drink at me and downed it in one long swallow. Then he sat there sniffing at the rim of the empty glass, looking behind me at the rows of books, the piles of newspaper clippings, the photographs of my wife and daughter. I suddenly remembered my wife saying, just after we'd gotten married, that she would divorce me if I ever went into politics.

"Using that blade sure as hell won't help you live on," I said.

"Won't help you much either," he replied, and he laughed – the same demented chortle I remembered from his childhood, but now with the added momentum of a chugging gut and wagging brown braids. I thought he was going to asphyxiate himself, but finally he took a breath. This seemed to calm him. He sat there silently for a few seconds, as if reminiscing. Then he stood up abruptly.

"Guess it depends how I use it," he said. He loomed over the desk, sighting along the knifepoint, aiming it at my face. I leaned back in my chair, but not before catching a whiff of the foul emanations of his breath. He swept his arm across the desk, pushing my drink, my newspaper, my Waterman pen set, my blotter, and my Caucus briefing books in an avalanche on the floor. Then he threw his own glass over the edge for good measure.

At this point even the geriatric security guards seemed like potential saviours, but I was leaning too far back to reach the emergency buzzer with my knee. I was at his mercy. He took the knife in both hands and stabbed it down into the desktop in the corner near my left hand, and then he dragged the blade across the surface to the other corner. It sounded like a zipper opening. Sweat dripped off his nose onto the wood. He joined the other two corners with a similar line, forming an x on the surface.

He stepped back to admire it for a while, and to catch his breath. I didn't know what to say. The knife was still quivering, but he seemed suddenly lucid. He lifted his gut away from the front of his jeans, pulled a leather sheath partway out, and slid the blade back into it.

"My name is Badger King," he said. "Remember."

That was all. He glared at me for a moment, and when I didn't respond, he pulled the chair out from under the doorhandle, unfastened the lock, and lumbered out into the hall. I didn't follow. I leaned forward in my chair and ran my hands along the furrows he'd cut into my desk. The fibres of the wood were raised, like a message in Braille.

I could have called the cops after Badger's little visit, and they probably would have put a restraining order on him, or maybe even charged him with assault or uttering threats. They tend to take it seriously when someone points a weapon at an elected official. It's bad for democracy. But I had already ratted on him once, and I couldn't bring myself to do it again. He had done no real harm, and I thought it was unlikely he would threaten me again, now that he had aired his grievances. So I told no one about our meeting. I requisitioned a new desk and tried to forget the whole incident. Still, I was nervous enough that I started carrying a knife of my own, a five-inch folding Buck that I kept in the pocket of my suit. Sometimes, when I was alone in the office, I would open that knife and trim my nails, admiring the way the blade gleamed in the light of my desklamp.

FOUR

I didn't see Badger for a long time after that, though I heard he was back in Champlain, and that he had assembled a little gang of malcontents who got together once in a while to complain about the general shittiness of their lives. The people there apparently accepted him in his new identity, though I doubt if they could see much difference between Francis Cameron and Badger King. The only difference I ever noticed was that he didn't make his living from drugs anymore, though I'm sure he would have tried if the market hadn't already been flooded and the supply routes well-established. He *did* go on welfare, just as I had predicted, and he moved in with Marie King once again. And, according to my sources, he spent a great deal of time in the pool hall, regaling people with remarkably inaccurate stories about Guevara and the Sandinistas and Riel. The only people who took him seriously were his dim-witted henchmen, none of whom had more than a grade five education. I knew that for everyone else up there, it wouldn't be long before the novelty of Badger's reappearance wore off, and then they would stop listening to him altogether.

In any case, I far was too busy with my own career to worry about Badger's activities. The Premier appointed me to Cabinet in November of that year, and I was suddenly faced with an endless stream of stakeholder meetings, strategy sessions, interviews, and speeches. I had to hire half a dozen staff members, and I had to learn everything about the Department of Economic Development and Tourism. It was as if someone had pressed the fast-forward button on my life: for those first three years in Cabinet, I was scurrying from one event to the next, seven days a week. Not that I minded. I thrived on it. I was damn good at it too – so good that I attracted billions of dollars of potential investment during my time as Minister. And the crowning glory of my achievements was the Barraconda Project. After months of whining, cajoling, palm-greasing, and backroom threats, I succeeded in doing what no one before me had done: I attracted a megaproject to the Windfall riding. It was, really, the deal of the century. It would mean high-paying jobs, untold prosperity, pride for the people. I would be re-elected forever. What more could a politician want? I was the envy of all my colleagues on both sides of the house. The opposition members who complained about environmental regulations and feasibility studies were only resentful because they hadn't thought of it themselves when they were in power.

The Barraconda Project was what I had been dreaming about since the earliest days of my political ambitions. It had the potential to transform my homeland, to bring real wealth and self-respect and even some political influence to the people of the north – people who had been mired in poverty since before I was born. This was the whole reason I had gone into politics. So when the deal started coming together, it was only natural that we should devote our remaining energies to planning the announcement ceremony. We spent weeks on it. Vince always referred to it as "The Announcement," as if it was the next best thing to the Annunciation. I think he really saw it as an elaborate church service, dedicated to the god of lucre, with myself in the role of high priest. I knew he was prone to overenthusiasm, but I found myself playing along with his exalted visions of The Announcement. After all the work I had done, I felt entitled to a little exorbitance when it came time to take the credit.

I'll never forget anything about that day. It began with my first flight on a private jet, along with the other dignitaries and spouses who were to take part in the ceremony. I tried to disguise my amazement at the opulence of that machine. It had yard-wide leather recliners instead of airplane seats, and there were six built-in computer terminals, a four-foot video screen for presentations, and a gas-burning grill for Mr. Mendacio's steaks. He ate tenderloin once a day, to keep himself regular, he said. He also wore identical black hand-tailored suits every day, with only the slightest variations in the pattern of his ties to alert you to the fact that he had indeed changed his clothes since the last time you'd seen him. He had two assistants, one for his itinerary and another to communicate his ideas to the proper people in the company to get things done. This ideas assistant was forever punching notes into his hand-held computer. As the president and chairman of Diversified Development Trust, Elmore Mendacio was not interested in details. He was a grand schemer. He didn't let himself get bogged down by the drab and constricting realities that the rest of us live with. "Reality is an excuse," he'd said during our champagne breakfast just after takeoff. "It's what little men invent to cover up their inability to dream." Vince had thought this so profound that he'd scribbled it on the cover of my Announcement briefing book.

It was like a legislature cocktail party at thirty thousand feet. Near the front of the cabin, Mr. Mendacio held court with the Premier and the federal Minister of Mining and Technology, Gerry Lalonde. They nodded and chuckled and shook their heads in unison, like a synchronized dance routine. I talked golf with Oliver Caldwell, the CEO of Barraconda Nuclear, which was a subsidiary of DDT. Since he would be in charge of the construction and daily operations of the reactor, I made an extra effort to be charming. Dozens of my relatives had already been hounding me to get them jobs at the construction site, so every bit of goodwill I could accumulate with Oliver would be useful later on.

Vince sat in the back with the rest of the entourage, all of them rifling through briefcases and comparing itineraries. He was still involved with the last-minute planning of The Announcement, trying to ensure that there would be enough streamers, balloons, and beef-on-a-bun for every man, woman, and child in the district. We'd hired a special-events company to take care of these things, but I wanted Vince to be sure it was done right. We needed a lot of local flair, with little girls throwing flowers, old ladies displaying their beadwork, and maybe some traditional powwow dancing. Every media outlet in the country would be represented there, so it was our one big chance to put Dog River on the map.

I had bought a new Italian suit for this occasion, and had gotten my hair cut at 5:30 that morning. This was going to be my first appearance on the national news, and I wanted it to be memorable. All of Rita's family in Saskatoon were going to watch for me on TV, and my father-in-law had said he would tape me on his VCR. Vince had briefed me on all the statistics: two point three billion dollars invested, twelve-hundred full-time jobs not counting the expected three-to-one spinoff factor, a new value-added market for the nearby uranium mines, the possibility of selling power to the States for megabucks. And above all, it gave my people, a historically downtrodden group, a huge opportunity to stand up for themselves and be proud.

This was the first time a jet had ever landed at the Dog River airport, and the runway was nearly too short, but the pilot managed to get us stopped before the edge of the tarmac and take us back to the delapidated hangar building, where dozens of locals were waiting for us, led by the mayor, Joseph Kisanwakup. I could see from my porthole window that Joseph was wearing a tie, as I had instructed him. He knew this was his big day too: the reporters would be asking him what he thought about having a nuclear power plant built in his town. I had personally gone over his lines with him for several hours the previous week, and I'd been able to reassure the Premier that we would have nothing but glowing comments from Joseph. True to that promise, Joseph looked the picture of gratitude, welcoming the plane with open arms, rallying the assembled townspeople into a spontaneous cheer that I was sure would make the evening news. There was a row of television cameras beside the hangar to document it all.

None of the chiefs of the local band councils had arrived yet, but I knew they liked to make their own entrances, so I wasn't surprised. They had all agreed privately in meetings with the Premier and myself that this project was good for their people. And, to sweeten the pot, Diversified Development Trust had volunteered to make generous yearly payments to each band council so every reserve could build new skating rinks and recreation complexes. I'd always had difficulty dealing with the chiefs, especially Elvis's father, Narcisse Sasakamoos. But this time I knew we had them onside. It was a win-win situation for everyone.

We stepped out of the plane to a lovely smattering of applause, Mr. Mendacio first and then the Premier and then the rest of us. It was a perfect June day: nearly cloudless, with a slight breeze to cool things down. The turnout at the Announcement would be phenomenal. Everyone in town and half the neighbouring townspeople would be there, and all of them would remember this day for the rest of their lives. I almost cherished the memories in advance, having gone over this event so many times in our planning sessions that it seemed like it had already happened. All the credit for this would go to me. We had seen to that. I imagined that some day, in one of the new subdivisions of Dog River that would inevitably be built, they would name a street after me.

We went through the grand routine of handshakes and smiles and introductions for about twenty minutes, and then the entire group of us went on a tour of the town, led by the surprisingly gracious Joseph Kisanwakup. We had rented four convertible Cadillacs from Saskatoon, and all the v.i.p.s rode around in them, waving like the Pope. We crisscrossed town, from the gymkhana grounds to the school, the hospital, and even the dormant hockey rink. It was like being in a parade with only four floats. Old folks waved to us from their gardens and front porches, and preschoolers tagged along behind, hoping to smear their fingerprints on the paint of a genuine Eldorado. Rita was with me in the car, and she seemed happy about my involvement in politics for a change, perhaps even proud of me for having brought the light of prosperity to a place that she had never liked. I suppose she thought a big enough injection of money would transform Dog River into a northern version of Saskatoon.

The kids had all been given a holiday for the occasion, but some of them were at the school when we arrived for the tour. We ate pemmican and bannock prepared by the kids, and the bigwigs were presented with elaborately beaded mukluks and beaver-skin mitts. I had seen this kind of pageantry in Regina, when diplomats and trade delegations visited the legislature, but I had never imagined it could occur in Dog River. My dad and all my brothers and sisters had driven up from Champlain to watch the spectacle unfold. The only people who couldn't make it were Uncle Pious and my mom. He was sick with the flu, and Mom had gone out to his place to make sure he was following the doctor's orders. At his age, you had to be careful, and Mom knew from long experience that the word careful was not in Uncle Pious's vocabulary.

The final destination of our miniature parade was the ball field, where the crowds had been building for an hour already. Vince was so worked up by this time that I had to give him one of Rita's sleeping pills to bring him back down to earth. Even so, his thoughts were flying from one thing to the next, and he was running back and forth through the crowd, talking on his cell phone and scribbling notes to himself. I was beyond nervousness. I could feel the momentum of the day building, had caught the magic of self-confidence in that rising energy, and I knew I would perform brilliantly. Bring on the fanfare, I said to myself. Bring on the drums. When the Premier and Mr. Mendacio had reached a lull in their handshaking, I caught their attention. They both nodded that they were ready, so we all assembled at the back of the ball field, behind the concession. I signalled to the bandleader and he started the band in a rousing and joyous march. We walked up through the middle of the crowd, all of them standing up to welcome the procession of their economic salvation. Mr. Mendacio, Oliver Caldwell, and the Premier were in the lead, comprising the trinity of our new religion. Most of the chiefs were there, and as far as the others went, to hell with them, I thought. They could kiss their skating rinks goodbye.

I was the Emcee, so I brought up the rear of the parade and waited until all the dignitaries were standing at the front of the stage before I went to the microphone. As I stepped up to speak, there was a flood of applause, begun by Vince, who was standing near the candy floss machine, clapping with idiot intensity. I waited for the sound to abate. The nylon banners on the podium were fluttering in the breeze, and the arrangement of yellow roses near my left hand was brilliant in the sunlight. I looked out across the former ballfield at the rows of people on the lawn chairs and benches we had provided. There were twice as many people as seats, and the overflow had to find places on the grass. Near the back, a congregation of teenage boys stood in a circle, ignoring us – probably passing around a joint. But everyone else was watching me. My people. I had never so completely held their attention, their admiration, as I did at that moment. Everyone was silent now, but I still didn't speak. I took a deep breath, savouring the scent of the roses, savouring also the people before me: their lumberjack shirts, baseball caps askew, sunglasses, fluorescent clothing on the youngsters, permanent-pressed green trousers on the old boys, flouncy print dresses on the young mothers. They were a sad lot, marked by their failures and the failures that came before them. But still they were capable of hope. And I was here to deliver.

"My friends," I said, feeling my voice leap through the loudspeakers, reflect off the crowd, and echo in the surrounding field. The cameras were focused on me, a whole bank of them to the right of the stage. Everything would be preserved.

"This is a great day for Dog River, and for all the peoples of the North." I felt them move involuntarily closer, as if to learn a secret. "As you know," I continued, "your governments have been engaged in negotiations with Diversified Development Trust and Barraconda Nuclear for several months. You may have heard rumours about these negotiations. You may have heard only part of the story. We are here to give you the truth."

That word rung in the air, echoing back and forth across the field. The crowd murmured, and several of the TV cameras swung from me toward the people, to document their awe.

This was when the explosion hit. I think I was the first to notice it, though many of the cameras caught it too. It was not exactly a mushroom cloud – which was most certainly the intent – but rather a marshmallow cloud, a huge amorphous blob of dust that sprang up silently out of the field half a mile behind the concession. The people couldn't see it. Their eyes were all on me, and I had no time to warn them before the sound waves hit. In that microsecond between the flash of the powderkeg and the arrival of the noise, I saw with inexorable clarity that all of our plans were going wrong, and that I was utterly helpless to do anything about it. Then the people all leaped simultaneously into the air, as if the explosion had occurred beneath them instead of behind them. This vision of collective surprise might have been comical in a different place and time, but now it was a nightmarish choreography, performed for my benefit alone, as if audience and entertainer had switched places.

I clung to the podium and managed to stay on my feet, but the blast bewildered me for a moment. There was a pulsing sensation in my ears, an internal aftershock that throbbed in my skull. The people had collapsed into a monumental heap of humanity, a single being that flailed erratically with hundreds of limbs and exhaled a hideous many-mouthed cry more terrifying than the noise of the explosion. It seemed like they had been welded together into an accidental monster that would scuttle across the ballfield to devour me. I shrank away from them involuntarily, and as I turned I saw that the v.i.p.s had fallen too. Rita was on her hands and knees, looking down at the plywood between her palms as if searching for a contact lens. Manny Brighton and his wife and Gerry Lalonde and Oliver Caldwell were splayed across the stage, entangled in upended chairs. The Premier and Mr. Mendacio had jumped against the stage backdrop, and had toppled onto the grass with it, covering the words "Partnership" and "Development" with their bodies. The Premier's wife was the only one still seated, but it seemed that she had lost consciousness, since her head was slumped forward against her chest like a sleeping pigeon.

As I tried to absorb the meaning of this spectacle, the throbbing in my head intensified. It was joined by a shrieking dissonant whistling sound that went through my ears like a spike, and suddenly there were two dozen white creatures circling in front of the stage, flailing at drums, blowing into silver whistles, holding orange megaphones up to their masked faces. They were naked, with ghostly white paint smeared all over their bodies, and the masks were black wooden semicircles with mutations and tumors hanging off them in all directions. Electrical wires sprouted from the tops of the masks, and the eyes were camera lenses.

And there, up on the stage leading them, was Badger King, his belly swaying to the rhythm of the drums, his whitewashed penis waggling at the crowd. The mask did nothing to disguise him. He pointed a megaphone at the people and chanted "DDT IS DEATH TO ME! DDT IS DEATH TO ME! BARRACONDA LET US BE! BARRACONDA LET US BE! "

As soon as I saw Badger, the whole bloody nightmare suddenly made sense. My bewilderment coalesced into an adamantine hatred, a gleaming vengefulness that propelled me into action before I could think about the consequences. I leaped over Gerry Lalonde's prone body and connected in midair with Badger's left shoulder, sending the megaphone spiralling onto the grass. He collapsed under me, and when I got back up on my knees, I punched him hard in the mask, my knuckles glancing off the wooden buboes that clung like barnacles to the right cheekbone. Agony blossomed across my hand and crept slowly up my wrist. I was sure I had broken something, but the pain only made me more determined than ever to exact my retribution on the meddling demon beneath me.

"I'll kill you!" I screamed. "I'll kill you!" And I leaned over his belly to reach for his throat. He kneed me in the groin, but not before I got my thumbs to his windpipe. The mask flopped from side to side as he twisted to escape. My suit was smeared with his white paint, but I didn't care. I crouched over the mask and stared into the mismatched lenses where I thought his eyes would be. I pushed my thumbs in further and felt something break.

Then I caught a reflection in those mask-eyes, a brief ghostly image that loomed on the convex surfaces as Badger arched his neck in pain. I hesitated. Badger thrashed feebly beneath me. I thought I'd seen lenses – not the ones on the mask, but other ones, wide as portholes, with people huddled around them. I forced myself to look up, and saw what I had already begun to dread: a dozen cameras trained on me like gun barrels. I looked up into them, and then beside them at the earnest faces that gazed at me expectantly, like spectators at a boxing match. These people had no intention of stopping me. They wanted me to go further, to throttle every last pro-testor. It would make a better story for the news.

I stood up, almost drunkenly, and the cameras all swung upward in unison. Then the microphones bristled at me out of the assembly, and the questions started. I didn't understand a word, but I had no intention of answering them in any case. Before they could come any closer, I leaped over Badger's legs and fled down the side of the ballfield. My instinct was to hide myself in the crowd, but even as I dodged behind the first astonished cluster of my constituents, I realized that would be impossible. I was only a few steps ahead of the fastest reporters, and besides, everyone in the whole place knew me. I prayed, vainly, for anonymity. All I got was more attention, as people in the crowd stood up to watch me dragging a trail of reporters and cameramen behind me like a desperate Pied Piper.

I ran past the makeshift concession and past a dozen of the dope-smoking boys, who were still lying on their backs and gazing blankly at the sky, unsure if the explosion had really happened or if they'd just managed to score some particularly potent stuff. I was pulling away from the reporters by this time, but seven or eight of them were still in question-asking range, and I knew I wouldn't be safe until I was out of sight. I kept running, despite the horrid clenching sensation in my lungs, the icy abrasiveness in the back of my throat.

When I reached the edge of the parking lot, I saw the four stately Cadillacs parked over by the gate, and I headed instinctively toward them. Sure enough, the third one still had the keys in the ignition. I vaulted into the driver's seat, cranked the keys, and roared out of the lot before the reporters could figure out what was happening. I saw them for a few seconds in the rear-view mirror, standing in the middle of the lot with their microphones hanging limply and their tongues lolling in breathless exhaustion. Then the Cadillac's trail of dust obliterated them and everyone else from my view. The whole ballfield melee seemed to disintegrate, as if it had been a dream or a movie scene. Fresh air cascaded over the windshield and funnelled into my oxygen-starved lungs. I could almost think straight. I began to believe I had made my escape.

Yes: I left the Premier, and Vince, and my wife, and all of

my astonished constituents, to fend for themselves with a horde of rabid reporters pursuing them. It might have seemed callous to some (it did to Rita), but I knew even then that I had no choice. Anything I said to the media would certainly be used against me. If we wanted to have a chance of preserving the Barraconda deal, I had to find somewhere to hide until the whole bloody thing had blown over. I raced around the outskirts of town for a few minutes, to confuse any reporters who might still be following me, and then I turned south on 496. There was only one place I could feel safe. Uncle Pious's.

I lived in his root cellar for seventeen days.

FIVE

It was a surprise to everyone that the Premier kept me in Cabinet after my role in the Barraconda debacle. I became a magnet for bad publicity. Images of me attacking Badger King were standard fare in the papers and the TV news programs for weeks after the event. When I finally came out of hiding, the reporters were waiting like wolves. Environmentalists also despised me with a truly frightening intensity, and they conducted regular protests at my office and even at my house. The *Leader-Post* printed a poll that said fifty-four percent of the respondents believed I should resign my Cabinet post (only sixty-two percent knew who I was). But still I refused to do it. I thought I could salvage the Barraconda deal, and knew if I did, I would be a hero again. I couldn't let Badger put an end to my career so easily.

The Premier wanted to fire me of course, but in the end he

only demoted me, taking away the Economic Development and Tourism portfolio and leaving me with the Northern Affairs Secretariat. He was universally criticized for doing this, especially by certain ambitious government MLA's who wanted my place at the cabinet table. However, as I explained to him in some detail, he really had no choice. I was the only government member who was from the north. Furthermore, I was still popular in my constituency, and the Premier knew he was going to need every safe seat he could get in the next election. Strange as it may seem, a lot of my constituents were actually happy to see me on TV strangling a protestor; to them it meant I was fighting for jobs and for progress. Knowing this, I suggested to the Premier – tactfully – that if I was no longer in cabinet I might have to run as an independent in the next campaign. I also pointed out that if I was put in such a position, it would be my public duty to expose some of the questionable practices that I had witnessed during my time in government. I gave him a list of these backroom transgressions, all of which would certainly hit the news-stands like bombs. He considered my modest proposal for a few seconds and then he looked me in the eye, trying to decide whether I was bluffing or not. I wasn't.

"You son of a bitch," he said. "Don't expect another favour from me."

I remember thinking there was a hint of admiration in his voice.

Yes, I played hardball, and it saved my political skin, but

unfortunately my victory brought with it a number of unpleasant consequences. It meant I had to stay in the public eye while I was ridiculed from every quarter. Reporters smirked at me in the hallways of the legislature. When the House was in session, the Opposition heckled me with gleeful savagery. In Question Period, they asked me question after question, even though my miniscule portfolio had no serious issues to deal with. They only wanted to put my face on the evening news once again, to remind the electorate that I had not been stripped of my responsibilities. They howled for my resignation. One of them even wrote a song about "Kenny the Killer," which they chanted in the background while I was trying to answer their malicious questions. If Vince hadn't been staring down at me from the gallery, mouthing the word "calm" to me like a hypnotic mantra, I would have proven them right by jumping across the floor and strangling every last member of Her Majesty's Loyal Opposition.

Even my own colleagues started avoiding me because they didn't want my tarnished image to rub off on them. Manny Brighton, who used to drink with me at the Diplomat four or five nights a week, developed a sudden burning interest in his ten-year-old son's hockey career, and he told me he had to spend every night at the rink. Whenever we talked at the legislature, he was shifty and nervous, as if he thought we could be ambushed by reporters at any moment. Some of the other Government members refused to speak to me at all. At

Cabinet, I was basically frozen out of the decision-making process. And speaking of being frozen out, my own wife clamoured for my resignation more forcefully than any of the Opposition critics. She didn't go public with her disapproval, but sometimes I thought she would. She believed that the only way to end our humiliation was to quit everything and move as far away as possible. I couldn't explain to her that politics is about survival, and that the people would forget all about my shortcomings when the next government crisis came along.

This turned out to be true, though Rita never acknowledged it. Within two months of the Barraconda incident, a series of new scandals began to erupt. Some were the ones I had mentioned to the Premier in our private talk. There were allegations of kickbacks in the Transportation Agency, and questions about some of the Ministers' travel expenses. A leaked document indicated that a computer whiz from Montreal had bilked the Planning and Priorities Committee out of seven point three million dollars with promises of a miraculous computer program that could translate laws from English into French. There was a new crisis like this every few weeks in the fall and early winter of that year. None of these scandals involved me, so I quickly faded from public perception.

Unfortunately, there was also a great deal of bad news during this period, which precluded the possibility of optimism. It was gratifying to see some of my colleagues taking their turns in the hot seat, but their screw-ups started to affect the polling results in my own riding. Even though my constituents still trusted me, they were getting tired of the government's incompetence, and I was worried that they might vote against me just to get rid of the ruling party. An even more acute problem, though, was that the Premier had been serious when he'd said I couldn't expect any more favours. This meant he didn't go to bat for me when Barraconda started getting nervous about the bad publicity in Dog River. I think they could have been persuaded to continue with the project if the Premier had been willing to provide some extra incentives, or even just some moral support, but none of this was forthcoming. For all I know, he may have actively dissuaded them. I pestered Oliver Caldwell as much as I could, but it was no use. By the sixteenth of September the deal was officially dead. They tried to be cagey in their announcement, talking about exploring other options and reassessing their land-base strategies, but the reporters called it like it was, and the headlines read "Barraconda Falls Through." My credibility in the riding was instantly called into question. I heard from Elvis that Badger and his cronies threw a week-long party when the news of the broken deal reached them. I think they were still celebrating their victory two months later at that fateful party near Hope Falls, where Badger consumed a smorgasbord of intoxicants and then drove north into a blasting storm to meet his appointment with oblivion.

You'd think the loss of the Barraconda project would be a severe enough punishment for me, but the Premier had a sadistic streak. When the pre-election porkbarrelling started in earnest, none of my requests were answered. I was faced with the prospect of running a campaign without any of the benefits that government members can usually expect. There were no new schools or hospitals for me to open, and none to promise for the future. No tax breaks. No sod-turning ceremonies or agreements-in-principle. Not even the hope of a feasibility study or two. I may as well have been in opposition. In fact, I would have been better off as an opposition member, because I wouldn't have had to work against the crescendo of anti-government sentiment that was building throughout the province. When the election was finally called (the Premier waited until the last possible date) our polls showed that I was neck and neck with the socialist candidate Agnes Desrosiers, who had come out of nowhere to gather a surprising amount of support. It was going to be a real battle, and I knew I couldn't rely on any outside help. Still, I was confident that I had a good constituency organization and a solid core of voters in the north. Those two things had got me through my previous elections, and I thought they would probably do the trick for me again this time. The province-wide polls made it fairly clear that the government was going to fall, but I had stopped caring about that, since the Premier had done nothing for me. The only thing I cared about was winning my own seat.

Except for the incident at Badger's shrine, which I've already recounted, I don't remember much about the campaign. I spent the whole three weeks living out of the van, rocketing from one event to the other and repeating the same tired slogans every time I opened my mouth. But one thing I'll never be able to forget is the election night. I still replay it in my mind, trying out different interpretations, wondering what else I might have done. Some things happened that night that I've never told anyone about. I'm recording them here because I want the people to know what I was really up against in that election.

I remember coming back to campaign HQ with Vince after my six-hour recuperative nap. The polls were already closed. The phone banks against the north wall were empty, the dog-eared voters lists hanging down from each phone, the pages torn and stained with coffee. The names were colour-coded according to the door-knocking we had done, which told us whether a particular household supported us or not. The job on election day was to be sure that all of our supporters got to the polls. Volunteers worked all day phoning people, pleading with them to go out and do their public duty. The problem in a riding like Windfall, where the incumbent is well-known and the challenger is a nameless parachute candidate, is that the incumbent's supporters tend to get complacent: they assume you will win, and they decide not to waste their time voting. Governments have fallen as a result of this phenomenon. We

weren't about to let it happen to us. We offered polite remin-
ders, rides to polls, and even stern coercion when necessary.
With a few of the old codgers from the Whispering Pines
Nursing Home, we damn near marked their ballots for them.
You can be sure Iron Agnes and her lot did the same when they
had the chance.

The crowd of volunteers cheered as I entered HQ, and they
all surged toward me, reaching to shake my hand, thumping
me on the back, grasping my shoulder in congratulations. I
was in a daze, but I kept my smile glowing and I squeezed the
hands as firmly as I could. I'd been sick with a mind-numbing
flu ever since the tri-party debate in Windfall the week before.
It happened to me every election, so I had come to expect it,
but that didn't make it any easier. I felt like an imposter in my
own body, giving the impression of confidence and strength
when really I could hardly stand up, let alone think. Vince had
been conducting me through the final week of electioneering,
priming me every morning with caffeine pills to counteract the
stupefying effects of my Sinutabs, then forcing me to memo-
rize platitudinous phrases which I was to regurgitate into the
microphones of all reporters, no matter what questions they
asked me. *Less government means lower taxes. We're committed to
providing the best health care in the world. Buy low, sell high.*
Whenever I gave a speech, he stood at the back of the room
making hideous faces to keep me from falling asleep in mid-
sentence. If I had to walk more than ten steps in any direction,

he kept a hand on my left shoulder to prevent me from weaving. Without Vince at my side, I'm sure I would have collapsed the moment I stepped in the door of the HQ. I didn't have the constitution for politics, though I would never have admitted it back then.

Vince led me toward the back of the room, parting the crowd with circular motions of his hands, as if he was doing the breast stroke. I drifted along behind him, past the stacks of election pamphlets and the extra lawn signs that were propped against the temporary partition. In the back, my campaign manager, Ashley Montague, was sitting at a makeshift plywood table with a phone receiver in each hand. He was trying to punch numbers into his computer at the same time. When he saw us, he gave me the same false smile I was giving him.

"Good work, men," he said. "She's all in the hands of God and good judgment now."

I glanced at Ashley's computer, and saw that some of the preliminary poll results were already starting to come in. I didn't try to figure out the numbers. Vince sat me down and went out to find me some coffee. Ashley repeated some numbers back into the left-hand receiver. I put my head down on the table. The last poll we'd done had given us thirty-five percent and Agnes thirty-six, with ten percent for the Liberals and twenty-one percent undecided. The margin of error was five percent. It could go either way.

Of course that poll didn't reflect what had happened at the

candidates' debate, where by all accounts I was the clear victor, despite the impairment of my faculties. By the time the damn thing was over I had managed to promise a new hospital, an elementary school, and tax breaks for the middle class. These were more concrete promises than Agnes's vague fiscal alchemy, and they seemed to hit home with the voters. Of course I had no authorization to make such promises. But nobody challenged me on those grounds, and the Premier must not have cared, if he knew at all.

Vince gave me a huge mug of coffee, then stood between me and the computer screen as he studied the results. "Why don't you go out there and join the troops," he said. "It might do you good." We all knew we were going to lose the town of Windfall, and nobody wanted me to see the numbers until the rural and northern polls started reporting.

"All right," I said. A couple more phones rang as I was making my way past the partition, and Vince grabbed both of them.

The volunteers were talking in small groups, nursing coffees and Cokes and cigarettes. In a way, my flu was a blessing; without it I'm sure I would have started smoking again. Luckily, in my state of infection, everything tasted like burnt potatoes, no matter how appealing it might otherwise have seemed. Also, the flu so dulled my mind that it saved me from the stress that would probably have worked me up to Vince's level of anxiety. As it was, I could relax in the clouded protection of my stupor, even though I was running a dangerous fever and had to stampede to the toilet every hour to let loose a volley of diarrhea.

My infamous election posters were plastered on the walls. This was the face that so many of the socialist horde had kicked, spat on, and spun their tires over in the past two weeks. We'd never seen anything like this election for sign vandalism, especially in the north. The only thing to do was take the moral high ground, report everything to the cops, and put in new signs. I had never liked the photo they used of me on those signs, and was certain that I hadn't approved it. Somehow it distorted my patented crowd-pleaser smile into a leer. I looked like someone you might *want* to drive over with your truck. But by the time I saw the posters there were already four thousand of them piled in the office and it was too late to order new ones.

I was sure the poster screw-up had something to do with Jarvis McConnell, but I couldn't say anything about it since Jarvis's dad was the biggest contributor to my campaign. When Ralph McConnell offered the services of his son for the election, I didn't realize *I* was doing *him* the favour. Ralph was a contractor, and he didn't want Jarvis working for him because the kid cost too much to keep around. When he fucked up, he did it big. Ralph figured it was cheaper if he just paid Jarvis to stay away. So my campaign headquarters became a day care centre for a nineteen-year-old geek who passed the time by shooting flies with elastic bands. In the meantime, someone had spat copiously on my picture in the front window, and nobody'd bothered to clean it off.

Jarvis was at the blackboard now, wearing a hand-puppet of John Diefenbaker, holding a piece of chalk in the puppet's hands and using it to draw up a chart with spaces for the poll results: "We," "They," and "Lib." He treated the election as an elaborate card game. I suppose it was one to him. He would make his way back to his father's construction company one way or the other.

"Hey, Kenny," he yelled at me, waving Diefenbaker in the air so the puppet's jowls shook. "You want to lay odds on the results?"

"I'll bet you my job," I said. Smart-ass.

Several campaigners from the youth wing of the party were exchanging stories beside me, studiously ignoring Jarvis. It was their first election, but they spoke like seasoned veterans, telling each other how they had converted socialists right up until the doors of the polling stations had slammed shut. They were slightly embarrassed of me, but they let me stand with them for a while so that I too could escape Jarvis. They asked about my health, and I lied; they asked about the province-wide polls, and I lied; they asked about the local polls, and I lied again. Finally I saw my wife and daughter entering at the far end of the room, and I excused myself. They were wearing matching, though not identical, black-and-white wool suits with glossy black shoes. On Rita, my wife, it looked stunning, but on six-year-old Rachel I had to admit it was overkill. Still, I was in no condition to argue about wardrobe. I was just glad that they'd come at all. Rita had made a rare showing that morning, when she'd served coffee to the volunteers for about three hours. I was satisfied with that; it gave at least the illusion of spousal support, which was about all I could ask for. Her father had been a Liberal MLA in the sixties, and she claimed it had driven him to drink. So any interest she showed in my political career was grudging to say the least.

"I brought your sinus pills," Rita said when we met in the middle of the throng. Jarvis had just begun to write the first set of numbers on the board, and everyone was standing on tiptoes.

"Vince gave me some too," I said. "I think I've taken too many already."

Jarvis and John Diefenbaker wrote: Lib: 715, They: 2,236, We: 2,014. The crowd was silent at first, but then Ashley yelled out from behind the partition, "Those are our weakest polls! The rest are the strong ones!" Everyone cheered, and the crowd pressed in around me, touching me on the arm, the back, the shoulders, as if I was a faith healer and could do magic by my touch. I got carried up by it, forgot Rita's calm and slightly disapproving presence, and revelled in the attention. Several people kissed me, men and women. I cut myself loose from the tension, allowed Vince and Ashley to take care of everything.

Some of the youth members got into the champagne we'd hidden for the victory party, and they gave me a plastic cup of it. I downed it and seemed to gain some energy from the bubbles. I talked on and on about God knows what, and everyone listened attentively. Soon someone gave Jarvis another piece of paper and he erased the earlier numbers with the back of Diefenbaker's head, then grabbed the chalk with the puppet's hands and transcribed the new numbers:

Lib: 1,143, They: 3,988, We: 4,007!!!!

This time the cheer lifted me right up off the floor. I'd never felt such euphoria, even during the relatively easy victories in my two previous elections. I laughed at somebody's joke about how do you find a needle at an NDP convention. I tried to tell one of my own but got mixed up, and people laughed anyway. Then Vince was in front of me, trying to herd me into the back room.

"What is it?" I said.

"It looks good," he said, his arm around my back. "Only four more polls to report, and they're all in the north."

He pointed to one of the televisions in front of the partition. The information was passing below the announcer's desk, poll by poll: Castanega: NDP: 647, LIB: 201, PC: 866, Spoiled: 11; Pine Point: NDP: 362, LIB: 334, PC: 744, Spoiled: 17. When the TV declared me "Leading," there was another shout, and more of the champagne came out, plastic corks bouncing off the ceiling and into the crowd. The room was indeed crowded now, and all kinds of people I didn't recognize were shaking my hand and helping themselves to the champagne. I flashed a smile at Rachel through the crowd, and then Vince and I made our way to the back room for the final tally. It would be more effective if I and my family didn't come back out until the final numbers had been announced. Then the people would be able to focus on us in our glory, a happy family united in the service of the Party.

When I got to the back, Ashley only had one phone cradled to his neck, and both hands on the keyboard. I sat down on the desk beside Jarvis's video game machine. We'd allowed him to set it up there in the hope that it would keep him occupied and prevent him from damaging anything else. I sipped on my second or third glass of champagne. Even Cordon Brut tasted vaguely like burnt potatoes on my influenza-ridden palate, but the texture of the bubbles was soothing in my throat. Ashley had stopped typing and was verifying the numbers. He seemed to be having difficulty believing one of them.

"You're sure it's two hundred and twelve?" he said. "How the hell could that be?"

"Two hundred and twelve what?" I said. He held up his hand for silence, and turned away from me.

"Uh-huh. Okay. Well, I don't see how, but still. We've got enough. I better get on the horn to Elvis and see what's the final count up there. Yes. Kenny's right here, and he says to send his love. You better hurry on down here for the party. All right then. Drive safe."

He spun back around in his chair and started dialling another number, glancing over at the TV screen and then at me.

"That was your sister," he said. "Spoiled ballots. Don't ask me how, but the people of Champlain have forgot how to mark a goddamn x on a piece of paper."

Vince brought Rachel and Rita into the room, and they stood around Ashley's chair, trying to decipher the numbers on the computer. Ashley reached around his phone cord and tweaked Rachel's nose.

"We've still got enough, though," he added. "Your Dad's gonna be a champ!" he said to Rachel, who was holding her hands over her face for protection. "As soon as I get ahold of that damn Elvis, it'll be official."

Rita was leaning forward to give me a congratulatory kiss, but Vince stepped between us and shook my hand with manic glee, wrenching my body so fiercely that I spilled half my champagne down my left pantleg. I didn't care. I was going to win. If we were still ahead and Dog River was the only poll not reporting, Iron Agnes didn't stand a chance. The socialists had never been strong up there, even after the failure of Barraconda Nuclear. All we had to do now was wait for Elvis to report, or for Agnes to phone over and let us know she was conceding.

As I was mopping myself off, Rachel asked if she could play *Stealth Bomber* on the video machine. I didn't know how to switch the damn thing on, but finally Vince figured it out and gave her a chair to stand on so she could see the screen. Rita was watching the little TV beside Ashley's computer. She took some lipstick out of her purse and applied it delicately, holding the tube like a paintbrush.

"Where the hell is he?" Vince said.

"You know Elvis," I answered. "He probably thinks *we* should be phoning *him.*"

"I am," Ashley said. "No answer for the past hour and a half."

We listened to my daughter bombing Iraqi tanks, battalions, and nuclear facilities. "PULL UP!" the machine squawked, and she did, leaning back as if the thrust of the engines was real. On the other side of the partition, somebody opened another champagne bottle. The whole crowd laughed at something, probably more of Jarvis's antics.

"Dog River!" Rita said, pointing at the TV. We leaned over Ashley's chair and squinted at the numbers that moved like a train beneath the anchorman's desk. There they were: NDP: 452 LIB: 14 PC: 0 Spoiled: 870.

"What!" Ashley yelled.

"They reversed the numbers," Vince said. "It has to be a mistake. It is categorically impossible to spoil that many ballots."

The phone rang and Ashley picked it up.

"Murray," he said. Murray Michaelson was Agnes's campaign manager. Vince was already on the phone to the TV station, trying to straighten out the mistake about the numbers.

"No," Ashley said. "He hasn't reported yet. Yours?"

There was a long pause, and Ashley's eyes gradually narrowed until I could hardly see his pupils. Then he covered the receiver with his hand and said "Get Melinda."

Melinda Burns was the Chief Electoral Officer for the riding. I flipped through Jarvis's haphazard Rolodex and, miracle of miracles, found her number. As I was dialling it I heard Ashley say, "No, we do not. We do not concede."

He hung up and then reached for the receiver of my phone before anyone had even answered. Vince was still wrangling with somebody at the TV station. I had forgotten how much he whined in situations like this. Rita stared blankly at the TV screen. Rachel manouevred the joystick. Ashley had turned away from me and was speaking quietly into the phone. Finally he spun around in his chair and handed the receiver back to me.

"She wants to talk to you herself."

"Hello?" I said.

"Kenny." There was a wincing sound in Melinda's voice. She was a friend and supporter; I had appointed her to this position.

"I don't know how this happened," she continued, "but there were…irregularities. In Dog River. Eight hundred and seventy-one spoiled ballots."

My mouth tasted like iodine. Vince looked at me as if I

was radioactive, fatal to the touch.

"How?" I said. "How were they spoiled?"

"They all had a name written in at the bottom with an x beside it. I think you know what name."

In my delirium, I had no idea what name she was talking about. Then it came to me. It was so obvious I couldn't even muster any rage. Badger. He'd been in the race all along.

"No votes for me? Not even one?"

"The official report says zero. But with such irregularities, you can make an appeal...."

"Not even Elvis?"

"There is an appeal procedure. I have it right here in front of me."

I handed the phone back to Ashley, who held it out at arm's length for a long time without hanging it up. We all stared at our own separate patches of the room. Then Vince started to cry, and Rachel put down her joystick to go over and hold his hand.

"We loved you," Vince said to me, as if I was already dead and he was addressing my ghost. "We all did."

"Elvis," I said. "Not even Elvis."

Ashley announced the official results to the rest of the supporters, some of whom became drunkenly furious. Someone lobbed an empty champagne bottle across the room and it hit the front window, shattering the pane. Luckily the posters that were scotch-taped to the glass kept the shards from flying into the crowd. Crumpled, glinting images of my face dangled from the windowsill. Nobody even attempted to clean up the mess. A gang of youth members stormed out into the night to destroy NDP signs.

I made the herculean effort of walking down two blocks to Agnes's HQ, ignoring the half-hearted questions of the second-string reporters who'd been sent over to cover the loser. A cluster of supporters came with me, along with Vince and Ashley and Rita. When I got in the door, the TV cameras were waiting, their lights flooding into my dilated pupils so I couldn't even see where Agnes was. I stood there, dazed, at the threshold, and finally she came to me. I gripped her small dry hand, mumbled some words of congratulation, smiled my election-sign leer. She tried to disguise her elation, but it kept springing back into her features like an electrical charge. She told me I had run a fine campaign. I looked into her watery eyes for one more second, and I almost told her, "You're not the real winner." But instead I turned on my heel and blundered out into the darkness.

When we got back to HQ a handful of supporters were still there, drinking champagne and Crown Royal, watching the rest of the results for the province. The government had fallen – the socialists already had a comfortable majority, even with seven ridings still up for grabs. Everyone told me they loved me. My shoulders were wet from the tears of supporters. People phoned from Regina to offer their condolences and to lament the return of socialism. All those friends I'd made down there. Every one of them would be out of work. The Premier had won his riding, but of course he didn't call.

The party was devolving into a drunken pigshow, so Rita and Rachel went home with Ashley's wife, Leanne. I drank some Crown Royal and sat at a plywood table with a few of the hard-core volunteers and friends. Several of them said they were moving out of the province, since they couldn't deal with another socialist government. Everyone wanted to go to Alberta. There were piles of flyers on the table with pictures of me shaking hands, cutting ribbons, kissing babies, making speeches. My platform was outlined in boldface print: FISCAL RESPONSIBILITY, ECONOMIC DIVERSIFICATION, COMPASSION-ATE LEADERSHIP. A GOVERNMENT AS GOOD AS THE PEOPLE. YOU DESERVE IT. The whole thing seemed so ridiculous now, so futile. They did not deserve it. They were not good. My own people in Dog River and Champlain, the ones I had dedicated my life to serving, had betrayed me. They had lied. When my supporters had knocked on their doors, they had said they would vote for me. How could such liars expect their politicians to be honest?

And then there was Elvis, the Judas of this whole affair. After what I had done for his son. I would never again trust anyone the way I had trusted him. He must have told his father and everyone else up there that I was the one who had destroyed Badger's shrine. That would have given Narcisse Sasakamoos and the rest of the Badgerites enough incentive to mount a secret campaign on the dead man's behalf.

Elvis might even have been one of the vigilantes who drove around knocking down my election signs. Yet whenever I talked to him, he said that things were going well: Badger King was fading out of people's minds, and the issues of the day were more important than the memory of a foolish folk hero. And then Elvis himself must have written Badger's name at the bottom of his ballot, and marked an x beside it.

I had given them everything, and they had spat in my face, kicked me down, spun their tires over my helpless image. They had violated me. And I had invited it, turned the other cheek.

No more.

I stumbled past the partition and out the back door without anyone realizing that I was leaving. Vince had shotgunned a magnum of champagne just after he realized we were going to lose, and he'd passed out as soon as we got back from Agnes's HQ. Someone had dragged him out to the van to sleep it off. I wanted to talk to him, to tell him whose name was written on the spoiled ballots, but I knew it would be pointless in his condition. In any case, I couldn't bear to see the election signs plastered on the doors of the van. I kept walking down the back alley, past the dumpsters and piles of rotting wood and glistening cars. It was cool outside, with a damp night breeze that seemed to push me along. I crossed Third Avenue into the next alley and kept floating south, toward the hill. We were staying with Ashley and Leanne, since we had moved to Regina four years earlier and didn't have a permanent residence in the riding.

There was a dark copse of poplars leaning over the alley midway through the block, and when I passed into its darkness it seemed like I was entering a tunnel. I couldn't see my feet on the ground, could barely hear the scuffing of my leather soles against the gravel. At the far end of the block, where Fourth Avenue intersected, I saw the silhouette of someone standing beside a street lamp. It was a man, bulky and dark-haired, but I couldn't tell if he was facing toward me or away. Then I thought I could make out a face: a wide, coarse visage with two tight braids hanging down in front of the ears. I didn't say anything, but kept moving down the alley, through the darkest part and on into the mottled light that filtered through the thinner foliage. He didn't move, but seemed to be aware of me, seemed confident of an imminent meeting, as if he knew me well.

I stopped. There was a haughtiness in his stance, in the way he lifted his chin toward me.

"What do you want?" I said, not expecting an answer but needing to say something, to issue some kind of challenge. He didn't seem to hear. The sodium vapour light above him cast a corona of orange light on his glistening hair, but the details of his face were obscured by shadows. My intestines contracted, warning of another surge of diarrhea.

I would have gone closer to find out who it was, but I couldn't. I had to get to a toilet or at least to the bushes. I ran back into the covering darkness, and it felt so much better to run that I kept going, out across Fifth Avenue and further down to the back door of HQ, which was hanging ajar. I went straight in without looking back, and then I slipped into the bathroom. Relief came immediately. When I got out into the front room, I saw Ashley slumped over on the plywood table, a burned-out cigarette butt still wedged between his fingers. I sat down beside him and rested my cheek on a pile of flyers. But I couldn't sleep. I waited there all night, surrounded by the ruins of my political career, the rags of bright paper and the clusters of empty slogans comprising the remains of my life.

At about five-thirty Ashley woke up, the right side of his face imprinted with the houndstooth pattern of his sport-jacket. I was achingly, unbearably sober. I didn't want to look at the election posters on the side of the van, so I told him I couldn't find the keys. We walked all the way to his place, plodding heavily down the back alley, shivering and cursing in the chill morning air. When we passed one particular streetlamp, its feeble orange bulb winked out. I didn't say a word.

SIX

I kept a journal during my time in office, hoping to write a book some day about public life. It would be called *The View From Here*, referring to the magnificent view from my ministerial offices, but also to the dizzying perspective at the top of the political system. I wanted the people to understand what it was like to spend your life trying to appease a selfish, unruly, and illogical mob. Maybe if they could see what a hell they had made of my life, they would stop blaming politicians for everything and recognize that they, the people, are as culpable as their supposed leaders.

Fear is the basis of every political system, but only in democracies do the *politicians* fear the *people*. The most cunning and sensitive cowards, the ones who can channel their fear into acts of appeasement, rise to the top. I planned to write about this phenomenon in detail – naming names, pointing fingers, even lamenting my own part in the whole futile game. I would expose the childish fears behind each of the government's major programs during my time in office. My colleagues would not love me for it, but even more, the people would hate me, for forcing them to acknowledge their complicity in all the system's failures. I was willing to take that burden on myself, perhaps because, since the Dog River debacle, I'd begun to take a perverse pleasure in the scorn of the public. Call me Saint Kenny, patron of democracy and lost causes.

After the election, though, I shredded my journal, along with every other document I could get my hands on. It was partly just the hysteria of transition time that took hold of me and wouldn't let go until I was sure all my tracks had been covered. Everyone was doing it. Half a dozen high-volume paper mulchers were flown in from Ottawa, and the Legislature was a confetti factory for a week. Night and day, above the anguished cries and tortured conversations of defeated MLAs and their employees, the voracious grinding of those machines could be heard. Once-incriminating documents became as innocuous as snowflakes. Red-eyed political hacks tossed bags of shredded papers into the marble hallways like clusters of gargantuan balloons. One guy in Executive Council got his tie caught in a shredder and damn near choked to death. I thought of the Premier's best house-rousing speeches, the ones he used to deliver at Party Conventions and youth rallies, when he would build his patter to a crescendo and then suddenly stop, lean forward against the podium toward us and say, "We're each and every one of us making history." Now here we were, pulverizing it.

I had planned to save a number of documents, some for personal interest, others as a means of keeping something on my former colleagues, as a kind of insurance. The journal was to be kept for posterity, even if I didn't make a book out of it. I wanted something to show my daughter and later my grandchildren, so they could have the story from my point of view for once. God knows, the media never allowed me such a luxury.

As Vince was off jamming papers into one of those all-consuming devourers of truth, I sat at my desk, paging through journal entries, recalling the numerous crises that had come and gone during my nine years of public life. I realized with some shock that they weren't as earth-shatteringly important as they had seemed at the time. Even the Barraconda disaster didn't seem *so* bad, now that the worst had already happened. I had survived. I would now go back to my law practice in Windfall, devote myself wholeheartedly to Rita and Rachel, and tell the electorate to take a flying leap into the nether reaches of hell.

Since the time I'd been appointed to Cabinet four years earlier, I had taken to storing the volumes of my journal in a locked strongbox, which in turn was locked inside my file cabinet. I had told no one about the journal or about my plans for a future autobiography. These precautions enabled me to be brutally honest in my writings without any fear of reprisal or breach of cabinet secrecy. Now, with the fourteen notebooks full of my political observations spread out on my desk together for the first time ever, I felt suddenly free. I was no longer a politician; I was a person. Never again would I be an unthinking drone, tirelessly repeating the party line. I could publicly acknowledge all the mistakes I felt the government had made, could even document those blunders in embarrassing detail, could issue harangues and disquisitions without fear. The previous nine years became, for the first time, my own.

It was while paging through one of the three volumes that dealt with the aftermath of Barraconda that I encountered a startling piece of information. I was sipping on a Crown Royal, leaning back in my chair, and gazing out onto the florid gardens arrayed like a mandala below me. Beyond my closed door, Vince's paper shredder wailed. I moved through the entries describing the Blind River demonstration, and then the newspaper clippings and photos of me strangling the masked figure of Badger King. Some of those photos fluttered out onto the floor and I left them there. I flipped ahead a few pages to the entry for September 3 of the previous year:

> *Mendacio says DDT wary of negative publicity.*
> *They're not going to build it. Just looking for a*
> *way out. Premier won't throw any more $ into*
> *the pot. Won't even talk to me, thinks I betrayed*

*him by throttling Badger King. What was I sup-
posed to do, shake the bastard's hand?*

RESOLVE. Do something about Badger. A.S.A.P.

This was a fairly routine indictment of Badger King. The surprise was the barely legible scrawl in the right-hand margin: Ratbone 668-3268 his mother's. $10 G now & 10 later?

Basil Alphonse Duprey. Ratbone. The murderer I had defended in my second year of legal practise. He'd told me he was guilty, but I'd gotten him off. The Crown's prime witness had been afraid to testify, and the rest of the evidence hadn't been sufficient for conviction.

A surge of diarrhea twisted my intestines. I took out my fountain pen, unscrewed the top, and poured a pool of ink onto the page, over the scribbled note. I closed the notebook. A bead of ink swelled out of the paper and bobbed there on the edge for a moment before splashing on the blotter. I didn't reopen it, fearing that the spot I'd made would remind me of something I didn't want to know. In first year psychology I'd taken a Rorschach test, and half the images had looked like skulls.

I sucked back my drink, then leaned over to the credenza and pulled out the bottle. There is something about the shape of a Crown Royal bottle, the crenellated edges and gemlike encrustations of the glass, that gives me solace. I poured another glassful and sat with the bottle between my legs. Still, the intestinal churning persisted. There was no telling where else I might have written Ratbone's name or made some kind of reference to him. The only sensible thing to do was shred the whole works.

I stood up slowly and walked through the outer office toward the file room, where Vince was still shovelling paper into the machine. I carried my drink partway, but then, when I saw how the whiskey was shivering in my hand, I took it back to the edge of the credenza and set it down gingerly. The bathroom was suddenly the highest priority. Luckily I had my own private toilet adjoining the office; I ran for it and slammed the door behind myself with one foot as I struggled with my belt. Just as I sat down, an explosion of sulphurous liquid burst from my bowels. I flushed quickly but another attack came in seconds. I sat there in the harsh fluorescent light, staring at my ignominious reflection in the vanity mirror. My face was the colour of wet ashes, and my half-extended tongue was absolutely white. Whoever had designed that bathroom must have wanted the high and mighty to get a humbling perspective on themselves. It worked. To avoid my reflection, I leaned against the cold tile wall and stared down at my shuddering, goosepimpled thighs. Wave after wave passed through me, as if I were not the point of origin but simply a conduit, a gate from some foul and pestilential place into this world.

I must have lost consciousness for a moment, because the

next thing I remember is waking up with my head resting on my right knee. I felt remarkably healthy, aside from the swarm of tiny lights that arced across my field of vision like atomic particles. I got up, washed my face at the sink, then got my Diovol from the medicine cabinet and downed the last of it. I told myself to look at my body objectively. Although my recent attacks had come to seem more and more apocalyptic, they were in fact no worse than they'd been throughout my political career. I became almost businesslike, invoking the positive self-talk they teach you in those Neurolinguistic Programming seminars. SIDE: Study the problem, Invent possible solutions, Decide on the best one, and Execute. I went through the steps mentally while irrigating my eyes with contact lens fluid. Ratbone was the problem, and shredding was the only solution.

I strode through my office and directly to the file room, where Vince was absorbed in his grim work, surrounded by piles of newspaper clippings, correspondence, briefing books, cabinet information items, and bloated green garbage bags. To avoid the occupational hazards, he had stuffed his tie into his shirt. It looked like he was humming along with the machine, though I couldn't hear his voice. If he was, it was the most bleak and despairing song imaginable, the howl and sigh of a tortured spirit. He was taking the defeat even harder than I was, and with good reason. I could always go back to the law. He had to find a marketing job, and nobody in the new administration was going to hire him.

I switched off the machine, and suddenly the office was quieter than a union holiday. No lingering hint of Vince's voice in the air. He looked at me quizzically, a handful of cabinet memos poised at the mouth of the shredder. I took my expense account credit card out of my wallet, pressed it into his free hand, and said, "Why don't you take the others out to the Diplomat. I'll join you in an hour or so."

"Sure," he said in a tubercular voice. His whole respiratory tract was congested, from the paper dust or else from weeping. He was so exhausted he didn't even comment on my ghoulish colouration.

"You used to love that place," he said.

"Still do," I answered, clenching his tricep with one hand. Since election night, I'd found myself constantly reminding him that I was still alive.

I strode back to my office, sat at my desk, and waited for the employees to leave. The journals were strewn across the blotter, some of them open. I tried to remember exactly where, and in what state, I had left each of them. Was it possible that someone had come in here while I was in the bathroom, and seen something?

I reverted to negative self-talk, my true mode of existence. I am the most fluent curser I have ever met, and my specialty is whispered profanity – an art I perfected on the floor of the legislature, where the microphones are surprisingly sensitive. I strung together whole tapestries of silent curses, including several epithets that had once been reserved for Badger King. After three or four carthartic minutes, I heard Vince and the secretaries leaving. I raised my voice slightly, for a few concluding railleries, and then made peace with myself. I went to the outer door and locked the deadbolt, then towed the Shredex Pulveromatic into my office.

When I switched it on, the omnivorous titanium gullet growled in anticipation. I picked up one of my journal notebooks, tore out fifteen pages at a time, and fed them in. Bits of paper spewed out the other end, like chaff from a combine. I felt remarkably lucid. There was a rhythm to this work, a groove. You couldn't put too many pages in at once or you'd choke the machine. When I'd pulled out all the pages from the first book, I tossed the flapping husk of the cover onto the chesterfield and reached for the next one.

Nine years worth of words. It was like mulching my own body. I remembered the gargling sound Uncle Pious's meat grinder used to make when he stuffed in the venison for sausage.

I didn't want to think about meat. I was destroying evidence. It was a rite of purification, transforming tainted pages into immaculately indecipherable wafers. Absolving all my sins.

But, as Father Archambault used to tell us in Catechism class, you must acknowledge the truth of your sins if you are to receive absolution. "The truth will set you free," he'd said to me and Frankie Poitras when he accused us of stealing sacramental wine from the sacristy. We never did confess.

"Admit it, you son of a bitch," I said, though I barely heard myself for noise.

I would. I would admit it, this once – as I obliterated every last trace. My dealings with Basil Duprey had been real. Otherwise, why was I destroying a decade worth of observations, the only truths I had salvaged from my public career? And why else had I been forced to make exorbitant false expense claims in the past year, if not to pay off the ten thousand I had given Basil?

Yes. All the month of September the previous year, I had driven to different payphones in the city, plugged in a fistful of quarters, and dialled the number of Mrs. Rosaline Duprey. She lived on welfare in a hamlet called Eclipse, a few miles south of Windfall. Whenever her delinquent son was out of jail, he lived with her.

Seven times in a row, Ratbone himself answered the phone, and I hung up without saying anything. His voice was distant and muted, as if he'd lost the habit of speech. God knows he should have been used to talking on the phone: it's the only way they let you communicate with visitors in the maximum-security prisons. He'd been convicted of armed robbery, attempted rape, and manslaughter by the time I met him, and I was sure he hadn't gone clean since then. Any further convictions would have landed him right back in the P.A. Pen, where he'd spent his formative years.

I had vowed I'd give up if he answered again the eighth time, but of course he didn't. The old lady picked it up on the first ring.

"What?" she said, chewing on something crunchy.

"Mrs. Duprey, this is Jack Shade calling. I'm a friend of your son's, and – "

"He's here. He's right here."

"No, that's all right, Mrs. Duprey. No. I wanted to talk to you because I'd like to surprise him. You see? Basil did some work for me a few months ago, some real fine work, and I wasn't able to pay him properly. But now I can, and I want to surprise him. Make his life a little easier. So I need you to give him a message."

"Get away!" she shouted at Basil, the phone still clamped to her jaw. "It's for me!" The cord rattled against something as she lumbered away from him. She spoke again, more quietly. "He worked for you in jail? What the hell kind of work was that?"

"Well, yes, he did. Some drawings, you know, those ink ones he does. Well, he sold them to me, and I think I paid too little. I just want to make his life a bit easier now that I can afford it. So if you tell him to go on over to the schoolgrounds on Sunday morning early, he'll find a package under the merry-go-round, and that's for him, with my compliments."

She finally swallowed her noisy bolus, then smacked her

lips. "Merry-go-round. I'll tell him. Funny goddamn place for a present."

"Thank you, Mrs. Duprey. It's the surprise of it – like Easter, you know? I hope the gift makes both of you very happy."

"Yap. Me too, I hope so. I never met you ay?"

"Maybe some day soon."

"Yap. Well, we can always use a honest dollar round here. Not too proud. Not like some, that'd rather steal a dime off you than take a dollar's charity."

"Good then."

"Yap. Okay. Bye now."

I hung up, took a huge breath, and staggered back to my car, where I sat behind the wheel for a long time, replaying the conversation. Kids in loud cars circled the parking lot, arms draped out their open windows. It was astonishing how some things didn't change, while my own life had veered in such a frightening direction. But I didn't once consider abandoning my plans. The whole thing was decided already, by the idiotic fact that Mrs. Duprey had answered the phone.

It was Thursday night, and already after eight o'clock. No time to waste. I drove south a few blocks to a convenience store and bought a newspaper, a day-old *Calgary Sun*, just to confuse things. Then I drove down Albert Street and pulled in at the back of the Legislature, in someone else's parking spot. There were no lights on in my office. I took my calfskin gloves, an x-acto knife, and the newspaper.

I had already composed the message in my head, so all I had to do was hunt for the words and letters in the paper. Still, it took almost two hours of fiddling by the light of my desk lamp to cut and paste everything onto a virginal piece of photocopy paper:

> *This Is sErious*
> *$10 thouSand now and 10 after*
> *baDGer king has an accident, you get the money*
> *must look accideNtal and no witnesses*
> *DEAD*
> *second payment same place*
> *ps I have eVidenCe about garNet ClinE*
> *sHred this paper and eAt it*

Even though I'd gotten Ratbone acquitted of Garnet Cline's murder, everyone knew he was guilty. I was counting on that name to buy me some safety. I slid the note, along with 500 twenty-dollar bills, into an oversized manilla envelope, and locked everything in the strongbox with my journals. Then on Saturday afternoon I told Rita I had to speak at a Tourism conference in Swift Current. I drove all the way up to Eclipse, paying cash for my fuel so I couldn't be tracked by credit cards. It was one-fifteen in the morning when I arrived, and the town was like a boneyard, the unpainted buildings glowing in the moonlight. I had to grope around in the school-grounds, past the skeletal monkey bars and the looming trac-tor tires, before I found the merry-go-round. It was rusty and lopsided, the iron loops curving out like the legs of a crouch-ing spider. I stashed the envelope underneath, then stood up and looked out for a moment at the rutted, quackgrass-infested ball diamond, the rickety backstop. I had never felt so alone. As I turned to leave, I gave the merry-go-round a quick shove with my foot, and it screeched like a chorus of demons. I sprinted to the car and spun out of the parking lot before the sounds had dissipated.

It was a seven-hour drive back to Regina, but I didn't get tired. I was too busy talking to myself, trying to convince the real me that Jack Shade had never existed. He hadn't really phoned Mrs. Duprey, hadn't cut those words out of the news-paper, hadn't put that money in the envelope. He wasn't really driving back from Eclipse on a clear and distressingly normal Sunday morning. He was just a character in my dream, the dream I was having at that very moment, as I slept in the rock-hard bed in Room 29 of the Superior Motel in Swift Current.

Hard beds have always given me nightmares.

SEVEN

A month after the election, I had already moved back into my office at Clarkson Clarkson & Janvier in Windfall. I hadn't practised law since my appointment to cabinet four years earlier, but I was more than willing to get back into it, to keep my mind off the recent disasters if nothing else. My partners, John and Audrey Clarkson, were glad to have me back. It seemed like they'd been piling up the work for me ever since I'd left. I started in on the low-profile stuff – the wills and contracts and real-estate deals. I had a powerful aversion to the court-room, which my partners believed was merely a recurrence of the old first-time jitters. The fact was, I had visions of myself sitting on the other side of the rail, in the prisoner's box. All the clients in criminal cases had begun to remind me of myself.

My wife and daughter were still in Regina, even though Rita had been offered her old nursing job at the Windfall

Union Hospital. She said she wanted to stay in the city until the house sold, or until I decided to move back down there. She was certain I wouldn't want to live in Windfall, among the people who had rejected me. I had thought I wouldn't either, but when it actually happened I couldn't think of anywhere else to go. It seemed somehow appropriate, as an act of contrition. I was into self-punishment in those days.

I decided that Rita was embarrassed of me, just as she'd been mortified by her father's decline into alcoholism and crankiness after his constituents had returned him to private life. The old man's fame had long been a source of discontent for her, and his subsequent infamy was more than she could bear. She never forgave him for bringing shame to the family. Maybe she thought I would follow the same pattern. In any case, she had little sympathy for me, since she had predicted an ignoble end to my career even before it began. Her refusal to move back was a way of finally showing her disdain for politics itself, and for what she knew it could do to a person. Besides, she wouldn't want to be seen in public – and least of all in Windfall, which she hated – with the world's saddest joke, a defeated politician. And so, when I finally did quit politics, as she had been hounding me to do for a dozen years, she lost interest in the marriage.

I too lost interest, but for different reasons. First of all, I had developed the fatalism of a doomed man: I almost welcomed every new calamity, because I felt I had predicted it.

Secondly, my mind was too occupied with thoughts of Badger King to give me time for anything else. In the evenings I sat in front of the TV with cold pizza and Crown Royal, ignoring the screen, just contemplating what I had done.

I lived in a barely-furnished apartment across the street from the Whispering Pines Special-Care Home, which I had officially opened only three years before. Sometimes Ashley came over to the apartment and we talked about the good old days in the trenches during the first two elections. He never asked me about the possibility of running again. Maybe he wanted to try for the nomination himself. He was the only friend who ever dropped in, even though everyone in town knew I was back. Sometimes when people saw me in the streets they stopped me to ask why I hadn't solved this or that problem during my time in office. Unemployment. Poverty. Native land claims. Simple things like that. I told them to go cry on Agnes's shoulder. After a while, the word got out and people left me alone.

The worst of it was, I didn't really want to be a hermit. More than anything I needed to talk to someone, to get an outside opinion on my predicament. I thought about telling Ashley, but I didn't want to make him an accessory. The agonizing perfection of my torment was that I had to contain it within myself, had to brood and speculate without any points of reference. I couldn't be certain exactly what I had done. I had never returned to the merry-go-round in Eclipse, so I wasn't sure that Ratbone had gotten the contract at all. I didn't even know whether he could read. It was possible that the money was still there, or that someone else had found it, or that Ratbone had simply taken the money and disregarded the note. I wanted to see him, to ask if he had really done it. But I hadn't made the second payment, and I knew he'd just as soon kill me as answer questions. My anxiety became so intense that I was tempted to go to the police and tell them everything, put the whole question into their hands. But what if they found me innocent? I couldn't put my family through such an ordeal for nothing. Besides, I knew full well by then that the justice system doesn't really find the truth; it just believes it does. A few fallible people get together in a little room and decide for the rest of us what happened, and who is culpable. I couldn't bring myself to trust in the arbitrary convictions of strangers.

Sometimes I dared to believe that it really had been an accident. Badger was undeniably stoned when he left that party at Hope Falls, and his record of driving offenses and car accidents was longer than his arm. Statistically speaking, his death was long overdue. The problem, for me, was the timing: he died five weeks to the day after I'd delivered the package. It was hard to dismiss that as coincidence.

Many times, as I looked out my living room window at the Whispering Pines Special-Care Home, its brick and glass facade rising up out of the once-vacant lot to haunt me with the vanity of my past aspirations, I thought about the shadowy figure I had seen beneath the streetlamp on election night. I wished I had gone closer to him. The backlighting had obscured the features of his face, making identification impossible. In Windfall there were lots of men with ponderous bellies and buckskin jackets and braids tight as bullwhips. And my own state of mind on that night, exhausted and feverish and loaded up with Sinutab, coffee, champagne, and Crown Royal, made me a less than reliable witness. Still, there was something about his stance, and the way he held his head, that stuck in my memory like an icon.

The last week of October Rita sent me five boxes on the bus, containing my winter clothes and some personal effects I had forgotten when I moved up to Windfall. None of these things were necessities. She only sent them for the symbolism of it. I had been planning to drive down to Regina for a visit, but when I started unpacking those boxes, I knew I wouldn't be welcome there unless I was coming back for good. Two overcoats. Ten pairs of shoes. My favourite cut-crystal ashtray, wrapped in a pair of brown wool pants that had gone shiny in the ass. I hadn't smoked for eight years, but maybe she assumed I would start again. She also included framed photographs of my father and mother, and a new one of Rachel which was inscribed on the back in her best printing, "To Daddy with love always hope to see you soon. Your daughter." There was no message from Rita, not even a picture.

I wondered if she somehow knew about my dealings with Ratbone, if that was the real reason she was leaving me. It was a paranoid thought, of course, and I dismissed it almost immediately. She may well have sensed a change in me since the death of Badger King, and she may even have stopped loving me because of that change, but there was no way she could have found out about Ratbone. I had never taken any incriminating materials home from the office, and even Ratbone himself didn't know that I had hired him. Besides, if Rita had ever suspected anything, I knew she would have confronted me right away. She wasn't the clandestine type. Not like me.

I had just finished comforting myself on that account when I noticed a patch of baby blue cloth in the Safeway bag full of scarves and toques that Rita had packed under the photographs. I rooted through the bag and pulled it out: a crumpled lace garter, begrimed with dust, speckled with watermarks on the satin lining. At first I had no idea what it was doing there, but then I remembered: it was the one I had taken from Badger's shrine. I had never told Rita about it, had in fact forgotten it the moment I put it in my pocket. She must have found it when she took my pants to the cleaners. And she had kept it until now, without ever mentioning it.

I suppose she meant this as an accusation that I was having an affair, though that didn't occur to me at the time. Women don't actually wear that kind of garter, especially up north.

They're only novelty items, tasteless souvenirs of weddings and stag parties. To me, in my distracted state, the garter only represented the shrine, which in turn suggested my moral and professional failures. If I hadn't destroyed that shrine, I would have won the election. Elvis would have stayed with me, and Badger's little band of instigators would've had nothing to rally around. I'd always blamed Badger for everything, but now I had to admit that I was just as much at fault. I had antagonized him from the very beginning, had made him into the vile and vindictive creature he was. Just as he had made me into a murderer.

And yet, when I'd visited his shrine, the first thing I had done was to sanctify the crèche by removing that blasphemous garter. I couldn't have guessed, in that moment of benevolence, that only seconds later I would desecrate the whole shrine. Taking down that garter had been perhaps the only kindness I had ever done for Badger. I remembered how it had hung above the Virgin's head: not dangling there but spread out across three twigs so it formed a near-circle. It had been so carefully placed. Not merely tossed up into the leaves like you'd imagine teenage pranksters might do. The more I thought about it, the more I came to believe that the garter belonged in the scene. It gave the shrine a folksy charm, and a sincerity that the bare plastic statue didn't have.

Then I realized: it wasn't a garter at all. It was supposed to be a halo. I had thought it was obscene, when in fact it was a symbol of sanctity.

I've always had difficulty distinguishing between perversity and purity – which means, I suppose, that I may yet become a saint. I held the garter above my own head for a few seconds, looked in the mirror. *That* was clearly perverse. The garter was no halo in this context: it became an outlandish prop in some ridiculous party gag, and my face took on the same leering expression that had been publicized so well on the recent election signs. All potential saintliness aside, I had to admit I had a knack for profanation. I remembered the time Frankie Poitras and I stole an illustrated Bible from the rectory and drew genitalia on the picture of the crucified Christ.

Enough of that, I thought. I had done some horrible things in my life, but it was still not too late. I could begin my atonement by putting the halo back where it belonged.

I drove north in a reverent silence, aglow with the prospect of imminent redemption. It was a glorious Saturday afternoon, the sun distant but still coldly brilliant. The poplar and birch leaves had all fallen, and they swirled up from the ditches behind me, reanimated by the wake of the car. This was the kind of day that my father and Uncle Pious used to take me hunting partridges. I got my own gun when I was fifteen, a little single-shot .410 with a full choke. I couldn't hit a damn thing with it, would have been better off using it as a club. My father thought I missed on purpose because I didn't want to kill anything. Maybe that was true. Maybe I was a natural pacifist. I knew I wasn't meant to be a murderer.

Champlain was virtually deserted when I drove through. For about two weeks in late fall, half the town goes moose hunting and the other half goes fishing for lake trout. This meant that nobody would recognize me and ask uncomfortable questions. I kept going on 496, past Hope Falls, where the water had diminished to a sinuous white line that seemed to cling to the rock face. The familiar shrines and cairns stood guard on the roadside, their flags and ribbons more colourful than usual against the bare arms of the trees.

I was going too fast when I approached Badger's shrine, and I nearly lost control when I hit the brakes in the middle of the corner. How stupidly fortuitous it would be, I thought, to kill myself here and end up with my own shrine next to Badger's. But even as I thought it, I knew no one would build a shrine for me. A state funeral perhaps, and a monumental block of granite on the plot I'd purchased for myself and Rita at Woodgreen Memorial in Windfall, but no shrine, no coloured banners, nothing to mark the place of my departure. I didn't deserve to live on in the minds of the people like Badger did. After all, I had always distrusted them.

I drove past the shrine about half a mile to a place where the ditch was shallow, and I pulled off the road, as close to the trees as I could manage. Anyone driving by would think my car belonged to a hunter. I picked up the garter from the passenger seat and stuffed it into my pocket, then got out of the car and waded through the fallen leaves out to the road. There was a slight breeze from the south that carried the scent of decay, or rather fermentation – a pleasant smell of the old becoming new. The gravel chattered under my Florsheims, which in my zeal I had forgotten to change.

There were no signs on either side of the crèche this time, which was a relief. Maybe Narcisse Sasakamoos and all the other Badgerites were satisfied with having foiled the election, and had moved on to other mischief. The sign I had destroyed was gone too, or else buried under leaves. I didn't bother to look for it. I kept walking along the road until I could see right into the inner sanctum. There was the Virgin, gazing at me, arms outstretched. She seemed to have forgiven my past indiscretion. Her hands were anchored to the neighbouring trees by strings of multicoloured streamers, and her feet were now cemented into place, rendering her impervious to marauding bears and politicians. She was still halo-less, but seemed otherwise unharmed by my previous attack.

I wondered what had really happened on this corner. Had Ratbone forced Badger off the road? Or was Badger already dead before he got here, was his body simply planted in the car before it burned? *Must look accidental and no witnesses.* Death by fire was the most horrific end I could imagine. Even after death, it seemed a barbaric way to dispose of a body: flesh curling up, melting away. Then they grind up the bones so everything fits in the urn.

Someone had been walking recently through the leaves in the clearing, stirring them into little piles, which reminded me of the confettied remains of my journals. Evidence, if ever the pieces were put back together. I had heard of CIA operatives who specialized in reconstructing shredded documents. They used arcane algorithms and computer programs. That was why, after I'd fed the last page into the Pulveromatic, I had gathered up all the remnants, tossed them in the fireplace, and lit them. The total erasure of a thing always requires fire.

I walked toward the statue, looking down at my feet, avoiding those polyethylene eyes that seemed to follow me as I approached. I stopped when I came to the dais, which covered her feet to the ankles. Cement overshoes, I thought. Someone had written with a finger in the concrete: BADGER KING, 1954. No date of death.

I prostrated myself at the base of the shrine and prayed directly to the soul of Badger King. *I was afraid of you from the beginning because you brought out something terrible in me. But that's finished now. I'm here to make peace, for good this time. And to ask for your forgiveness.*

I opened my eyes, looked around the crèche. The Virgin was motionless, the breeze still rattled a few leaves down the roadway, the chickadees still twittered. The sun had declined into the trees, leaving a vibrant orange glow that trickled through the branches. I had hoped for something more, some indefinable change in things. But I knew that was foolish. I stood up, brushed the damp leaves from my knees, and took the garter out of my pocket. A branch – presumably the same one I had taken the garter from – extended above the Virgin's head, where her veil was folded back to reveal a glossy white brow. I stepped up onto her concrete base and leaned between her arms to reach the branch. I stretched the garter around the three now-barren twigs that had once held it, pushed it down as close as possible to the main branch for security, and then stepped back to inspect the result. It was indeed a halo, somewhat elliptical but angelic nonetheless. A radiant beatitude seemed to flood down the Virgin's face, into her billowing robes, out her fingertips and along the rows of streamers into the trees. Her expression of pious sympathy softened into a smile.

I was about to embrace her when I heard something behind me, near the entrance to the crèche. I hid myself behind the statue and peered out from the edge of her robe. Two people walking hand in hand, one of them holding something. The first to come around the corner was Marie King. The other, still clutching Marie's hand and carrying a galvanized aluminum pail with a Seven-Up bottle sticking out, was Elvis.

I cringed behind the Virgin's coattails, and the happy couple didn't seem to notice me. What the hell was going on? Marie must have been at least sixty, and Elvis wasn't even forty-five. He'd bought into the Badger King mystique in a bigger way than I could have imagined.

Before I could think what to do, I heard Elvis gasp. Everything was silent, even the leaves. I didn't dare look out.

"Is it him?" Elvis whispered.

No answer.

"I seen something in behind," Elvis said. "Badger! It's us!"

"Badger?" she called, and then whispered, "He never come there before. Always been off in the bush more."

The leaves rustled. "Badger?" Elvis said.

"Look, the halo," Marie said. "It's back."

"Holy Christ," Elvis said. The Seven-Up bottle clanked in the pail. "Kenny!"

I couldn't resist such an opener. I leaped from behind the statue, flinging my hands out to the sides and twisting my mouth into a snarl. Both of them staggered back. Elvis dropped the pail, and several apples and oranges tumbled out.

"Goddamn right it's me," I said. "Where is he? You made me think I killed him, for Christ's sake. And here you've been hiding the son of a bitch all this time!"

Neither of them spoke. They seemed transfixed by my presence. Old Marie's mouth was so far open I could see her upper denture plate, and her eyes, magnified by rhinestone cat-eye spectacles, were the size of a cow's. Elvis's face had unclenched for the first time since I'd known him: it was blank with surprise, and he looked like a different person. He deflected his gaze away from my eyes, focused on something behind me. I stepped toward him, pointing at his face.

"And you, you fucking traitor you. How long were you in on this? Since when did you start delivering food?"

Still he didn't answer, and didn't look me in the eye. I noticed, as I got closer to Elvis, that the old lady wasn't watching me either.

"What the hell are you looking at?" I yelled. She shrank away from me but didn't break her gaze. I couldn't stand it any more. I turned around, scanned the clearing behind the statue, and then looked further back, past the first few blackened poplar trunks to a small spruce tree about forty yards in. Standing beside that tree, in all his slovenly glory, was Badger King himself. The sun was completely gone now, but even in the twilight I knew it was him. That greasy face and those piggish, watery eyes were perfectly visible. His arms were extended toward us in a parody of the Virgin Mary.

As I started running for him, I thought how strange it was that he didn't have his chin out in his trademark "whatsittoya" gesture. Perhaps he had learned some humility. Even if not, I was going to teach him some. The bastard had faked his own death, just to make me think I'd murdered him. He'd understood that my conscience was my weakness. Had he cut some kind of deal with Ratbone? The branches flailed my face, burrs and rosebushes grappled at my legs, and the damp leaves slipped out from under my Florsheims, but I never lost my focus. I threaded through the trees like a fullback on speed, ploughing through the underbrush and leaping over stumps, gaining momentum by the second.

Badger didn't try to escape; he seemed to know it was pointless. He only stood there with an almost wistful look on that fat face, his arms still out as if expecting an embrace or a fight. I wouldn't disappoint him on the last count. It would be just like the old days in the lot beside the pool hall – except this time I would prolong it, give him a taste of the hell he had put me through. I dodged the last tree between me and him, then took the final five steps at a full charge, my legs churning furiously beneath me, lungs throbbing like gongs, arms straight out at the level of his throat.

And somehow, I missed. He must have sidestepped an instant before impact, and I kept going, headlong, tripping on my own speed. Thank God he hadn't been standing in front of a tree. I landed on my chest and slid about five yards, a mound of wet leaves building up under my chin. Before I had even stopped, I was back on my feet, ready for him. But he wasn't there. I ran to the spruce tree and circled it twice, looking out at the monotonous pattern of poplar trunks that receded into confusion in all directions except that of the road, where the back of the Virgin was the only visible figure. I could *smell* Badger, his unmistakable pong overpowering even the scent of the spruce needles. I looked down at the leaves for evidence, but couldn't find anything except my own footprints. It seemed impossible that Badger could climb a tree, but still I studied the poplar branches. Nothing. He couldn't have taken more than five steps in the time I'd been sliding through the leaves, and yet he had vanished.

"Badger!" I yelled. "Come here, you filthy son of a bitch!"

No answer. The forest was utterly silent. I ran back to the statue and found that, as I had suspected, Elvis and Marie were gone too. The only sign of them was a single apple resting awkwardly against the Virgin's concrete dais. I picked it up and winged it as hard as I could into the bush, where it glanced off a poplar trunk and disappeared in the undergrowth.

I looked back into the trees past the Virgin, whose skin seemed phosphorescent in the twilight. "Badger!" I said. "You want to live on, you have to pay the price. You can't play dead. Once the people find out you're still alive, it's all finished."

My answer to this was the sound of a car door slamming in the distance. I ran out to the road in time to see Elvis's half-ton burning a gravelly U-turn and screaming north toward Dog River. I couldn't tell whether Badger was in there with them or not. If anyone but Elvis had been driving, I would have given chase, but I knew he could lose me in minutes. The old Chevy sped down a slight incline for half a mile and then roared up the hill on the far side, lifting a roostertail of dust that hung behind like a contrail. The last moment I saw them, as they crested the hill, they hit an enormous hummock and launched into the air, all four wheels suspended, as if they might escape into the stratosphere.

EIGHT

Though I had missed my chance at revenge, I came to realize that I'd received something far more valuable that evening at Badger's shrine: my redemption. Since I – and two witnesses – had seen Badger, I could be certain I hadn't killed him. Not that I gave Badger the credit for my exoneration. It was highly unlikely that he had revealed himself to me on purpose. He'd gone to so much trouble to fake his demise, and besides, it was the most successful death since Jesus Christ. It had increased Badger's popularity a hundredfold, and had at the same time pushed me closer to insanity by the day. What more could a vengeful egomaniac want from death, especially when he didn't have to die for it? But still, despite his contemptible actions, I was so overjoyed at the proof of my innocence that I couldn't maintain my initial fury. I didn't exactly forgive Badger, but I was able to detach myself from his meanness instead of turning it back on him like I'd done all my life. We had both done terrible things to each other, we had both survived, and I was prepared to let it rest at that. I was tired of the inane circle of retribution.

For several days after I returned home, I gave off purity like a smell. I hadn't felt such elation since my first election win more than nine years earlier, when I had paraded around the constituency for a month with an imbecile grin on my face. My conscience was so perfectly disburdened that I didn't even consider revealing Badger's secret to the rest of the world. I knew it would eventually come out, and he would be put to shame, as he deserved to be. But I didn't want any part in it. I would let providence take its course. In the meantime, I vowed not to waste my new life. I wrote a long letter to Rita, admitting that politics had turned me into a callous and petty man just as she had predicted, but also asserting that I had changed now, and that I wanted to be back together with her and Rachel, even if that meant leaving Windfall. I phoned my parents and arranged to visit them in Champlain the next weekend, when we would all go over to the nursing home and say hello to Uncle Pious.

The first snowfall came on Hallowe'en, six days after my run-in with Badger and his friends. I had a feeling that if there was one day in the year when I would see my former enemy again, this would be it. He was bound to show up in an outlandish disguise somewhere in town, at a Hallowe'en dance or a bar. Maybe he would even be so bold as to wear the hideous mask that he and I had made famous at the Barraconda Nuclear announcement. Despite my new-found indifference to Badger, I wasn't anxious for another meeting. I feared I might lapse into my former furious ways, and perhaps kill him for real this time. So I turned down Ashley's invitation to the masquerade dance at the Windfall Golf and Country Club. Since Rita was gone, I had a good excuse to avoid public appearances.

When I left work there was already more than an inch of snow, and no sign of a letup. It was beautiful, despite the inconvenience for kids and party-goers. The sky had a closeness, an intimacy – as if you could speak to it, could broadcast your secrets without anyone hearing. The flakes fell like immaculate shreds of paper, covering the dreary streets of Windfall with a layer of new grace.

I stopped at Chico's Place for my pizza and then picked up a bag of dwarfed Mars bars at the Safeway in case I got any trick-or-treaters. On the way home, I passed several clusters of kids, hunched over in their snow-covered costumes, brandishing wands and muskets and phasers, continually peering into their bags of loot. The crêpe-paper crinolines of a little princess were melting away in the moisture. I wondered what Rachel was wearing this year.

On the radio, a psychic woman from L.A. was talking about teleconferencing with the dear departed. Ouija boards were out, it seemed.

After I parked the car, I grabbed my briefcase, my pizza,

the chocolate bars, and the new forty of Crown Royal I'd picked up at noon, and shuffled through the snow to the back door of my building. As I entered the apartment, I felt a sense of relief – even triumph – at having gotten through the day without seeing a trace of Badger. Since my redemption, it had occasionally struck me that this innocence was too good to be true. I had to keep reminding myself that I had nothing to fear from Badger anymore, now that I knew his secret.

I poured myself a Crown Royal and sat down on the couch with a few slices of pizza. *Return of the Living Dead* was on TV. It wouldn't have seemed funny a week earlier, but now it was hilarious. Mausoleums and charnel houses belched forth their hideous inhabitants like gothic volcanoes. Battalions of shambling corpses chased shrieking half-clad women around the graveyard. "The dead outnumber the living by ten thousand to one!" a professor howled as the zombies overwhelmed his car. We didn't stand a chance.

After my second Crown Royal I fell asleep on the couch, the remote control still clutched in my hand. I dreamed of snow falling softly on the shrine of Badger King, drifting around the Virgin's robes and settling on her dais, gradually covering her until there was nothing left but a huge snowbank with a baby-blue garter resting on the top. Badger came out of the woods, walked up the snowbank without leaving footprints, and put the garter back in his pocket. I followed him into the trees and was just about to stop him when I was interrupted. The telephone. I picked it up before I had a chance to wonder who it might be.

"Yeah?"

"Kenny. That you? I need help here."

I sat up, and the remote control tumbled from my chest onto the floor. I didn't say anything for a while. I listened to the slow, wheezing respiration on the other end of the line. I knew that sound, knew the voice too, but I couldn't be sure. I remembered the time, years ago in Champlain, when I had offered Badger some free legal advice.

"Yes. It's me," I said.

"I knew you would again, like before. They found a paper. But I won't talk. Won't talk one word unless you tell me."

"What paper? Where are you?" I said, but before the words were out I knew. This was not Badger's voice. It was Ratbone.

"I'm in jail," he almost laughed. "Like always."

I hung up the phone. I sat there for a minute, staring at a TV advertisement for age-defying lotion. Then I slid off the couch onto my hands and knees, following the telephone cord behind the couch. When I found the jack, I disconnected it.

There was no need to speculate on why Ratbone was back in jail. Someone had found the little contract I'd sent him, and now he was accused of murder. I would have believed him guilty myself, if I hadn't known that Badger was still alive. The police would be doing their utmost to pin everything on him now, and they would also be searching for the author of that note. The question was whether I could be linked to it. But I knew that was impossible. Ratbone would never have phoned me for legal advice if he had known it was me. He had only chosen me because I'd gotten him off a murder rap once before.

But whether or not he knew, the idiot had unwittingly implicated me simply by calling.

I switched off the TV and sat on the floor in the dark, groping on the table for the Crown Royal bottle. When I found it I held it to my lips and took a long pull, watching the bubbles rise to the base of the crown. Outside the snow was building up on the railing of my balcony.

Of course. I wasn't implicated in anything because Badger was not dead. What worried me more were the other connotations of Ratbone's incarceration. If he had known that Badger was alive, he would have told the police, and they would have checked it out before arresting him. If he thought Badger was dead, then either he knew nothing about the case or he really believed he had killed him. Either way, it meant Ratbone and Badger were not in collusion.

Then how had Badger known when to fake his death?

A wave of fear shuddered through me, from my scalp to my duodenum. Was it possible that Ratbone had really killed Badger after all? Had I fabricated my encounter with him at the shrine? Or – even worse – was he dead but *also* there at the shrine? The possibility had occurred to me several times since the incident. Maybe the thing I had seen was not Badger at all, but instead an after-effect. A spectre. Living on beyond the confines of his body. Waiting at the scene of his death to accuse his murderer.

I stopped myself. This was truly ridiculous. I was not the kind of man to indulge in tabloid superstitions, especially when the evidence was so clear. I had seen him, I had smelled him, I had come within two steps of his smug, repulsive, living body. We had breathed the same air. My mind at the time was absolutely clear – no alcohol, no Sinutab, not even an expectation of encountering Badger. I was the perfect witness.

Besides, they were bringing him food. One does not give food to a phantom.

There could be no doubt in my mind that he was still alive. Maybe the timing of his death *was* just a stupid coincidence. Or perhaps he was even orchestrating my current torment, with the willing help of Ratbone. Or else Badger had somehow managed to pull one over on both of us. To find out, I would have to see Ratbone myself, to learn whether he believed in his own guilt.

It wasn't too late to drive down to the jail and talk to him right away, but I was afraid to go outside. Instead, I moved toward the sliding doors of my balcony, sat on the arm of the couch, and stared out at the streetlamp on the corner, where a cone of falling snow was illuminated like a ghostly Christmas tree. No one was there, but I could wait. I rested the Crown

Royal bottle on my knee, sipped intermittently straight from the crown. It was almost timeless, my waiting, and the snow coming down inevitable as death. The lights in the nursing home went out one by one, until only the hallways were lit. The orderlies made their rounds, striding like zombies. When the Crown Royal was a third gone, half a dozen teenagers converged on the high school math teacher's house, three doors down from the nursing home. They soaped his windows, tossed rolls of toilet paper in his weeping birch. Somebody must have called the cops because a cruiser showed up a few minutes later, and the kids vaulted the backyard fence to escape. After the cops left, everything was quiet again. The snow built up under the streetlamp, almost filling in the tracks of the cruiser before another car came along. The Crown Royal was half finished, and I switched to coffee so I wouldn't fall asleep. I didn't want to miss him. A few times I lapsed into a semi-catatonic state which was nearly as soothing as sleep, but I kept my eyes open religiously. It was a miracle my contacts didn't bond to my corneas. At the first hints of dawn I became more alert, certain he would soon appear. But the streetlamp turned pink and finally flickered out just as the snow was finishing. Badger didn't show, even in the blessed light of All Saints Day.

It shouldn't have come as a surprise later that morning when Matt Percy, Staff Sergeant of Windfall's RCMP detachment, knocked on my door. I had been trying to work up enough nerve to go over to the jail and talk to Ratbone. I'd even put on my coat, and was wrestling with my toe-rubbers when I heard the knock. I looked through the peephole and saw his mustachioed mug peering back at me. He had a devilish way of squinting, as if trying to conceal something rather than to see. I took as long as I dared – about three seconds – to get my heartbeat under control before I opened the door.

"Matt," I said, standing back into the hallway to diffuse the scent of Crown Royal on my breath. "What can I do you for?"

"Kenny," he nodded. "I see you're on your way out – sorry to interrupt. I've just got something down at the station I need you to take a look at."

"Professionally?" I said.

"No, not really. Just a thing we need some help identifying. We've been asking all kinds of people. If you don't have time, you can stop by later."

"Oh, that can wait," I said. "Just groceries. I'll take a look right now."

"Dandy," he said.

When I reached down to pull up the heel of my toe-rubber, I nearly collapsed, but Matt didn't seem to notice. I inhaled sharply and stood up, holding my breath to keep myself together. I locked my door and followed Matt down to the patrol car, where another officer was waiting. Judging by the angles of the lines in his face, this man had never smiled in his life. He got out and shook my hand, introducing himself as Vern Sandstrom, and then he swivelled back toward the car, opened the back door, and slid in. He motioned for me to have the front seat, so I wouldn't look like a prisoner.

It was only a few blocks to the station, but Matt wasn't the type to waste time.

"You ever hear of a fellow named Jack Shade, Kenny?" he said, looking over at me as he wheeled us onto Fourth Street. He kept staring for so long that he lost track of the road, and the car wandered off the beaten path, ploughing through several snowdrifts. He floored the accelerator and brought us back on course.

"Can't say as I have," I said.

"Me either. Most likely he doesn't exist at all. But if he does, we're looking for him."

"I'll keep an eye peeled," I said.

"Good."

We drove the last two blocks in silence. Vern in the backseat had a notebook open on his lap, but I couldn't see what he'd written. Since I didn't know him, he was probably with a special investigations unit from Regina or Saskatoon. I wondered if he had a tape recorder hidden on him somewhere.

Matt pulled the cruiser into the parking lot, and we went in the back door of the station and down the hall to the interrogation room, which also served as a staff room and occasionally a prison when all the cells were full. On the table was a piece of paper carefully sealed in a plastic bag. I didn't look too closely, but I recognized the blocky, uneven lettering. Matt and Vern were glued to me.

"Any thoughts," Matt said, gesturing to the paper as he closed the door.

I stepped to the table and looked more closely, even though I knew what it said. Ratbone, the fuckhead, never could follow instructions. *Shred this and eat it.* What had he done? Kept it in immaculate condition, suitable for framing. Must have pressed it in the family Bible.

"Looks like some kind of schoolkids' joke," I said.

"Well, it would be a joke, except Badger King is dead."

"Are you sure?" I asked.

"Reasonably. It's interesting you mention schoolkids. This note was found in a schoolyard. Apparently. But when we got to it, it was in Basil Duprey's house."

I raised an eyebrow. I felt obligated to appear surprised at every little revelation. Though I couldn't seem *too* surprised, or it would look like guilt.

"You know him, I think," Vern said.

"Matter of fact, he phoned me last night," I answered. "From the tank here. But I didn't have time to take on his case. I defended him once on a murder charge, ten, twelve years ago. Other than last night, I haven't heard from him."

This was true, and I could see they believed it.

"We're still questioning him," Matt said. He threw his hat

on the table, then fished a pack of cigarettes out of his coat. He lit one and inhaled with a nearly orgasmic expression. They weren't supposed to smoke in the building, but I wasn't about to lodge a complaint. Vern stared at the bridge of my nose while jingling a huge ring of keys against his leg.

"He says he didn't do it," Matt went on, "but this note was found in his mother's house, along with forty-three hundred bucks and lots of new toys that couldn't be explained. The old lady's on welfare, you know, and her social worker started wondering where the VCR and all the new clothes were coming from. We start questioning Mrs. Duprey, she tells us a guy named Jack Shade or maybe Spade called her up and told her he wanted to give Basil a present. Funniest thing, she tells us she voted Conservative because she heard your voice on the radio, and you remind her of Jack Shade."

I had to laugh. Matt joined in, but Vern kept his reptilian composure.

"Public life," I said. "I'm glad to be through with it. People used to tell me the craziest things. Some of them could have sworn they'd seen me on Oprah, or at the U.N...., or even, God forbid, at the Public Service Employees Union picnic. They always think they recognize you – and they do, I guess, but not from the places they think. They hear you on a talk show, or a TV interview, or at a ribbon-cutting ceremony, and then later they believe it was somewhere else."

Matt looked embarrassed, and I could tell by his silence

that they had nothing on me. Not yet anyway. He flicked some ashes into his left palm, cradled them there.

"Had to ask, for the record," he said. "You understand." He paused for a second, looking up at the clock that showed military time: 09:44. "This Garnet Cline, mentioned in the note here. He was the one Basil murdered?"

"Basil was acquitted. I was his counsel."

"I see. Right. I knew that."

"And of course," Vern said, "it's just a coincidence that you hated Badger King."

I waited several seconds for my indignation to crescendo.

"I'll tell you what's a coincidence," I said. "It's a coincidence that I just saw Badger King myself, in the flesh, a week ago today. You're looking for his killer, but he isn't even dead."

They didn't speak for a long time. Matt's houndlike face turned red, except for the white tip of his nose. Vern kept shaking his head, looking down into the notepad open across his knees.

"I have two other witnesses," I said. "Elvis Sasakamoos, from Dog River, and Marie King, from Champlain. They were delivering food to Badger, and I intercepted them. They'll probably deny it, but they saw him even before I did."

"You should've reported it," Matt said.

"Should've taken a picture," Vern added, almost smirking, as if he'd cracked a joke.

I shrugged. "Just trying to be helpful. Trying to tell you

guys you're on the wrong track. You don't like it when the truth spoils your fun, do you? I suppose I'll have to bring him in here by the scruff of the neck before you'll believe he's alive."

"Yes," Vern replied.

"Jesus," I said. "You guys just weren't born to believe. Suspicion is a way of life with you. But I have a feeling a jury would see the burden of proof a little differently."

That was it. I had them. Unless they could prove that the body they had was Badger's, they couldn't pin anything on me – or on Ratbone either, for that matter. Both of them knew this. They'd only been hoping to trick me into incriminating myself. And since it wasn't Badger's body at all, I knew they'd have a hell of a time proving it was.

"Well, that's all I know," I said. "You've got the wrong corpse, or your corpse has the wrong name. Badger King is still kicking. He stinks like the dead, but then he always did."

They still didn't believe. What more could I do? I refastened my coat and backed away from the table toward the door.

"I'll walk home, thanks," I said.

"If you go out of town," Matt said, "just phone and let us know where you're going and for how long."

He was still carrying his handful of ashes, along with the cigarette butt he had ground out on the bottom of his boot. He dumped it all into his jacket pocket without even looking, then dusted off his hands.

"Is that an order?" I asked.

"No," he said. "Suggestion. And you might want to avoid talking with your friend Basil. So as not to make us suspicious."

I opened the door and stepped out into the hallway. "Got it," I said. I left the door ajar, but they didn't see me out.

The clouds were thinning in the east, enough to reveal the sun. The snow was supernaturally bright. It hurt, like sucking on a peppermint when your face is frozen. I walked on the unswept sidewalks, stepping in other people's footprints, my face half buried in the collar of my coat. I wasn't cold, but for some reason I didn't want people to see me leaving the police station. Not that anyone would think twice about it. Lawyers are always visiting clients in there. But what I really wanted, I realized, was not to be seen at all. Unseen but present, like Badger.

Just as I decided this I saw old Gustav Bendl out snow-blowing his driveway. He switched off his machine when he saw me, and called out a greeting, but I only nodded and hurried past the spot he had cleared in the sidewalk. Old son of a bitch. He'd said he would vote for me, but then he went fishing on election day instead.

I didn't feel as chipper as I would have expected, considering I had just gained the hammer on the authorities. There was something about the town, the rows of modest bungalows with half-rusted Fords and Chevys in the driveways, that made my smugness dissipate. Behind those doors, in those living rooms with TVs flickering or stereos booming, in those bedrooms with unkempt bedsheets, in those kitchens with greasy dishes and country songs whining from the radio, were the people. These were potential jurors. *We, the people....*

I knew the people too well to trust them. They had failed me once before, in the election. There was nothing to guarantee they wouldn't fail me again if I was ever brought before them to be judged. I had seen juries make appalling decisions, either because they didn't understand the law or because they didn't really care. They wanted to get back to their kids and their jobs, so they just decided one way or the other, with little regard for the facts. Their negligence became the truth: whatever they thought happened, must have happened.

Basil Duprey's acquittal was a horrifying example of this. *I* would have convicted him. But it wasn't my job to decide; it was my job to defend him.

I was innocent beyond a shadow of a doubt: Badger King was alive, and therefore I hadn't killed him. But unfortunately, as a former politician, I would have a hard time gaining the compassion of a jury. They might even find it in their hearts to decide that the nameless body the police had found in Badger's car was indeed Badger. Matt and Vern and the crown prosecutor might be able to convince them. And if the real Badger King managed to stay out of sight, I wouldn't have a shred of evidence to go on. Then where would I be, with all my blessed innocence?

The only solution was to hunt Badger King down and bring him to the authorities alive. I had no choice. I would move up to Uncle Pious's cabin and start following Elvis and Marie around, and eventually they would lead me back to him. Failure was unthinkable. There was no telling when I might be arrested, and after that I'd have to throw myself on the fickle mercy of the people. Again.

The sooner I got him, the safer I'd be.

And yet, when I got up here to the cabin and began my preparations, I realized there was something else I had to do in addition to the manhunt. Badger has weapons and friends and luck on his side. I'm willing to risk my life to prove my innocence, but if for any reason I don't return from my search, I still want the truth to be known. I have to leave a record, for the people, so they will know the real story of Badger King and me. That's why I started writing this. I've been at it for eight days, and now I'm nearly finished. When it's done, I'll leave it here on the kitchen table, and the first person who finds it will be obligated to make it public. In fact, anyone who reads this, I charge you on pain of death to show it to three others. That way the truth will out.

You may wonder why I care about the people anymore, after all I've said about them. It's because they remain my last hope. Perception is reality. If the people believe you're dead, then you *are* dead. But if they believe, despite the evidence, that you're still alive – maybe you live on.

LAZARUS

TUESDAY, JUNE 14
ST. JOSEPH'S BENEDICTINE ABBEY

This is not a confession. No direct line to the Almighty, no appeals for absolution. I will spare the Lord my attempts at honesty, because they aren't the same thing as truth. As soon as I understand the truth I'll be ready to confess, but in the meantime I can only do what the Bishop has sent me here to do: pray and rest and meditate, and stay as invisible as possible. This last humble duty would be easier if the monks could give me one of the hermitages on the south side of the abbey grounds, but for the moment all of these meagre dwellings are occupied – perhaps by other clergymen seeking escape from their parishioners. The hermit's life seems to be enjoying a renaissance these days. Maybe after lunch I can convince the Abbot to build a new subdivision of shacks in the northwest quarter. I'd like one overlooking the pasture, so I can watch the cattle grazing in easy oblivion as I wrestle with the question of what I am.

I count it as a blessing that the Bishop sent me here. Perhaps I'm even thankful for Father Remy's treachery in reporting my troubles to our superiors. At breakfast today a retired deacon was explaining the Church's doctrine that abbeys and convents do not exist in the world. They are a different space altogether, an alternate universe maybe. That might be why I feel like I've done a rope trick, climbing out of my former life into a new one where none of the old encumbrances apply. Such is my hope in any case, though I know that the dark shape of my own doubts has followed me here, and I worry that Lucius Drake's rumours of my so-called miracle could arrive at any moment.

As an extra precaution I have gone incognito, signing in under my dead father's name, pretending to be a civil servant like he was. No one has disbelieved me so far. The best thing I can do is keep to myself – which is why I want a hermitage. For now, I try to enjoy the place from the safest vantage points. I stay in my room during the day, or I walk out to a secluded prayer hut in the forest south of the barns. Even from these enclosed spaces I can sense the gardens ripening around me. The flowers are everywhere. And when I see the monks out in the fields wearing their coarse monastic robes as they hill potatoes or pick raspberries or uproot thistles, I could forget what century it is.

I could forget many things. But not belief. The belief of others, that is. It confronts me every moment, in the brassy tolling of the chapel bells, the smell of incense in the hallways, the very presence of these buildings. All of it rests on an unquestionable foundation of faith.

How do we know what to believe? I envy those who have no need to ask that question. They are either saints or fools, but both possibilities seem preferable to the agony of unknowing that inhabits me now. That night, three weeks ago, something happened between me and Lucius Drake, but even though I was there I don't understand it. I was a witness, but only in the legal sense. Lucius has become a different kind of witness, spreading his message around the countryside like an old time preacher. And Guadeloupe has disappeared. I'm left alone to decide the truth about what I've done.

Two years ago I married Lucius and Guadeloupe in a secret ceremony, and I have never forgiven myself. Father Remy had explicitly forbidden it, but I did it anyway, perhaps because I knew he disapproved, or else because I was intrigued by the thought of clandestine activities. The couple had been to Father Remy's office earlier in the day, pleading with him for a church wedding. They had already been married three days earlier in a civil ceremony at the Calgary airport, where they had met for the first time. She was a mail-order bride. Lucius had been looking for a wife for years, but no woman who had actually met him would consider it. Guadeloupe's parents didn't know any better. They sent her from Mexico because they had fourteen other children and they thought this one, the beautiful one, would have a better life in another place. She arrived in Calgary wearing her cotton wedding dress and toting a trunk full of burnished black pottery that her family had sent as a dowry. Only one small urn survived the trip, she spoke almost no English, and when she got to Immigration she saw her reprobate husband for the first time. She was eighteen years old; he was forty-six. He was also a lumbering, unwashed wildman who smelled of dogs and had never been to church in his life. He looked nothing like the pictures of American cowboys she had seen in the movie magazines that she and her sisters had adored like sacred relics. He was more like the villain in a Mexican soap opera. She embraced him politely but turned her head away involuntarily when his bearded mouth moved toward her face.

And then when she saw that the marriage ceremony didn't involve a priest, she began her prodigious weeping. When they came to me three days later the tears were still coming out of her, and she was so dehydrated that her face was wrinkled up like an old woman's.

This was the only time Lucius ever gave in to her demands. It took him a long time to figure out what she wanted, since they couldn't speak each other's languages, but eventually she made him understand that she didn't consider them married until it had been sanctified by the Church.

Lucius didn't understand the fuss, but he was so frustrated by
the weeping that he finally took her into town for a second
marriage. I heard them down the hall in Father Remy's office,
Guadeloupe sniffling and sometimes repeating a short prayer
in Spanish, Lucius demanding to have a wedding then and
there. Father Remy refused – which must have taken some
backbone, given Lucius's belligerence and his reputation for
settling scores. Father Remy said they would have to take a
marriage preparation course, which would take eight months,
and he said Lucius would have to consider converting to
Catholicism. There was a storm of shouting and foot-stomp-
ing and Spanish litanies, and I was beginning to enjoy the
trouble he'd gotten himself into, when the couple suddenly left
his office and appeared in the doorway of mine.

Lucius was a huge man, his head the size and shape of a
pumpkin, his limbs post-like, and his posture almost comically
malevolent. His face was lit with a permanent glowering, his
eyes inflated with amazement or rage, like a professional
wrestler on TV. But it wasn't Lucius who convinced me. It was
his tiny, rumpled bride, cowering under his arm and looking at
me through the film of her tears with an expression of unshaking faith. It was not supplication. She wasn't begging me for
help. She already knew I was going to help, and she was thank-
ing me in advance. I was so unnerved by her certainty that I
went along with it. Not then, not with Father Remy listening
down the hall, but later that afternoon, when he had already

retired to his bedroom with his customary magnum of sacramental wine. I was trimming the cedar shrubs in front of the church, and they came by in Lucius's ancient International half-ton. He stopped on the edge of the road and waited for me there, his bride staring out the open window with a sibyl's dark conviction. I put down the hedge trimmers and walked to the passenger door and opened it for her.

"Park on the other block so he doesn't see you," I said to Lucius, and he nodded and took off in a maelstrom of dust and blue smoke. Guadeloupe and I were left there on the roadside, and I didn't know what to say. She wouldn't have understood me in any case. But she placed her tiny hand on my elbow, and smiled broadly, so I saw the row of fillings on her lower molars. She trusted me. I led her into the church and we waited at the altar for Lucius.

I was too nervous to appreciate how ridiculous the whole scene must have been. Lucius standing at the altar in his workboots and jeans and plaid lumberjacket, looking up at the crucifix on the back wall as if it was about to tumble down upon him. He sniffed at the remnants of incense in the air, and stood with his hands in his pockets. He had bought a huge white cowboy hat in Calgary for the first wedding, and he wore it again now, brazenly, right up to the altar. When I told him he had to take it off, he cringed and glanced nervously at the crucifix again before prying the hat off his enormous head and placing it on the carpet beside him. In those surroundings, which must have seemed bizarre to an irreligious man like him, I was temporarily his master. He wouldn't look at me, only at the crucifix or else at the statue of the Virgin in her crèche beside the pulpit. He even seemed wary of Guadeloupe, since he saw that she too knew something about this strange and lurid place, and perhaps he suspected that she could use it against him.

I sensed the power I had over him, and it was so gratifying that I tried to prolong my preliminary instructions. Here was Lucius Drake, the scourge of Windfall – gambler, drunkard, criminal – trembling before me on the lowest step of the landing. I had to make the most of it.

"Mr. Drake," I said. "Your wife is a Catholic. You may not have known that yesterday but you know it now, and you're going to have to accept it. That's why I have a condition. I can't perform this service unless you make a solemn promise here before God that you will bring her to this church at least once a week to attend mass and to receive the sacraments."

He was confounded by this proposal. His forehead produced a fantail pattern of pudgy creases, and his eyes lost their focus, as if he was attempting some impossible computation. When no solution was forthcoming, he exhaled heavily and glanced over at his grinning bride, who had no idea what we were talking about.

"Okay," he said finally. "I promise."

"Before God?"

"I promise before God to bring her if she wants." He spoke haltingly, as if it was he and not his wife who knew only twenty words of English.

I went on with the ceremony then, at a frenzied pace, elated that I had humbled him. He repeated his vows in the same empty tone as he had spoken his promise. Guadeloupe knew how to say "I do," and she said it ecstatically and more often than necessary. Finally I pronounced the blessing on their union, in the slightly disapproving echoes of the empty church. I felt giddy with transgression and with the knowledge that I had extorted a bargain out of Lucius Drake. I watched their awkward kiss, feeling suddenly that it was perverse to be the only onlooker. There should have been a burst of applause at that moment, and a blinding crescendo of flashbulbs, but there was only the rustle of Guadeloupe's dress and a surprised moaning sound from the depths of Lucius's chest. I was embarrassed, as if I had been spying on the honeymoon suite, and I fled back into the sacristy without waiting for them to finish. As I moved down the dingy passage toward the rectory, I heard Guadeloupe calling out her thanks in Spanish.

I will give Lucius credit: he lived up to his promise, which is more than anyone could have expected. He never set foot in the church again, but Guadeloupe arrived every Saturday for seven o'clock mass. She sat in the front pew just below the pulpit, and then after the service she knelt next to me in the dark and said her confession in Spanish. This was our arrangement from the beginning. "In Spanish, *Espanol*," I said to her the first time. "God will understand." She often spoke for many minutes, and with loud defiance, as if she was wrestling with each sin as she pronounced it. Sometimes I understood a word or two, but after a while I stopped trying to make sense of the sounds and simply let them envelope me. As I came to know more about her life with Lucius, I began to think of her confession as a song, an epic hymn of pain and isolation. Sometimes I wept as I listened to the flow of her syllables. I couldn't imagine what her sins might be, that they could call forth such a deluge, wave after wave that encompassed me in sorrow. Most probably it was not her own sins that she was recounting, but those of her husband.

I came to depend on Guadeloupe, to look forward to the sound of her voice in the confessional. Maybe it was a kind of catharsis, or an exaggerated sense of compassion for someone so unhappy. But even more, I felt responsible for her. It caused me endless torment to know that I had made her suffering possible, but at the same time it put me in the gratifying position of being her confidant, the only person in the world whom she could trust.

I offered to give her English lessons after confession, and Lucius often allowed it, when he was off drinking or gambling somewhere and didn't want to bother picking her up. Sometimes we sat in the rectory kitchen reciting verbs until midnight, and several times I had to give her a ride back home because Lucius didn't come to get her at all. She never told me she was in anguish, but I could see it in her eyes, and in the way she was so extraordinarily thankful for even the most banal kindnesses – a cup of tea, a tin of cookies to take home. When I gave her an English Bible to practise her reading, she broke into tears, and then apologized half a dozen times for drawing attention to herself.

She gave other hints about her desperate situation too. Once she told me she had been having recurring dreams about a black wolf that followed her everywhere. It was a brief but terrifying scene, and she trembled when she described it: moonlight, and the river enclosed in fog, and the black wolf walking toward her across the water. "Like our Lord," I said when she told me, but she was certain it was not Him. "El lobo, he's eyes are shine like stone," she said, and pointed to the yellowed zirconium in her wedding ring. Since the first time she had dreamed about the wolf, she had been terrified to go near the river, which was only a few yards from their house. Lucius sometimes forced her to go down there simply because he knew she was afraid.

Gradually I learned more about Lucius's vicious temper, and his drinking, and the people he called his friends. She never said outright that he had done anything illegal, or else I would have had grounds to send the police in there and take her away. I should have tried it in any case, if they would have listened. Everybody knew that Lucius ran more than one shady operation, but he'd never been charged with anything except impaired driving. He didn't seem to fear the police at all. He ran moonshine to the men who worked at the pulp mill, among others, and he just sold it off the back of the truck like they used to do in the old days. Twenty bucks a gallon for everclear so potent it almost evaporated before you could drink it. The pulp mill boys lined up for it, but none of them ever drank with Lucius or even talked to him much. He was beyond their comprehension.

People were scared of Lucius because they thought he was crazy – which was not an unsupportable conclusion. He had earned an undying reputation as the district loony the summer he'd started his infamous Bird Zoo. It was seven or eight years ago. The highway near his place goes north toward the provincial park, and he must have thought he could capitalize on the tourist traffic, because near the bridge he put up a sign that pointed down the back lane toward his yard and said simply "Bird Zoo 1 mi." He has always considered himself an entrepreneur. He slapped together some makeshift chicken-wire bird cages in his front yard, and there he displayed his collection of bedraggled magpies, robins, grackles, and starlings, along with his prize attraction: a breeding pair of pheasants that he had taken from Lenny McKay in lieu of a moonshine debt. Luckily for the birds, a weasel put them out of their misery before the second year of the operation. This shut down the business even more effectively than the SPCA could have done.

Lucius's dogs were another reason that people shied away from him. He was known as "The Dog Man" because he owned at least a dozen of them in various states of mutilation, and they followed him everywhere in a pack. I don't know how they survived without him when he went to Calgary to pick up Guadeloupe. They were the walking wounded, each of them missing some essential part: an eye, an ear, a leg. He had more sympathy for canines than for any human being. People took their injured dogs to him, and he performed impromptu surgeries on the kitchen table. He was the best amputator, stomach pumper, porcupine quill remover, and general dog doctor in the district – better than any of the veterinarians, and best of all, he worked for free. Just for the love of dogs. As his reputation spread, people started dropping their lames and strays in his yard, and he always took them in.

Lucius had been The Dog Man for years already when Guadeloupe married him, and it was clear when she arrived that the dogs considered her a threat. They never attacked her, but sometimes they herded her around the farm like a lost sheep. She took it especially hard when she saw that Lucius was kind to them, because it showed her that he was capable of human feeling. She thought there must be something wrong with her, that he preferred to give his affections to a pack of maimed dogs instead of to his own wife.

There wasn't anything I could do, legally, until Guadeloupe was willing to leave him. I told her she was a landed immigrant now, that she had rights and didn't have to depend on Lucius for anything. I said I could take her away to a place where the bad dreams would stop. But all she said to this was "I am married." As if she had expected such a life from the beginning and was now resigned to it. To me it sounded like a reproach, because I had allowed her to marry him, knowing what I did. If I had refused, as Father Remy had, she probably would have gone back to Mexico.

Finally I became so distraught at watching her misery that I suggested she seek an annulment. I dared to hope that the marriage had never been consummated, though I was too embarrassed to ask Guadeloupe for confirmation of this hypothesis. Lucius was such an unappealing oaf that I imagined he was somehow beyond sexuality. But even if the consummation issue was a lost cause, I had come up with another loophole. There had been no witnesses at the wedding, and that was enough of a technicality to render it invalid in the eyes of the Church. A petition based on this obvious omission would make me look like an idiot before my superiors, but I was more than willing to undergo some ridicule to save Guadeloupe. Unfortunately she didn't want to be saved. She knew what annulment meant – she had obviously already looked it up in her little blue dictionary – but she shook her head when I proposed it, and looked up from her hands into my eyes. "They will take me away from you," she said. That ended all discussion of the matter.

I kept my silence for a while after that, but still I continued to worry. I watched her for signs of pregnancy. If she were to have a child, she would be linked to Lucius forever. The words I had recited at their wedding ceremony came back to me like a malediction: "You will accept with joy the fruits of your union, and you will love them, and baptise them in the Catholic faith, and raise them in accordance with the laws of the Church." I wished I had left room for another loophole. Of course I couldn't tell Guadeloupe myself about the hazards of pregnancy, but I asked one of the ladies from the CWL to talk with her about the natural methods of family planning that are sanctioned by the Church. She never did have a child, so perhaps those arcane rituals worked. Or maybe her barrenness was the one consolation that the Lord sent to mitigate her suffering. A miraculous non-conception.

Unfortunately, the state of Guadeloupe's womb was the only thing in her life that could be considered miraculous. During the second year of her marriage, her situation stabilized at a particular dull level of pain and indignity, and she seemed to be moving through her life like a sleepwalker. She ceased to be amazed by Lucius's brutishness, his anger, his drinking. It all began to seem normal to her. I knew this was the most dangerous time of all, because it was possible that she might give in and become like him. She might lose faith in the Church and in me. So I told her to fight against him, to stand up for her rights, to do everything in her power to change him instead of allowing him to change her. I admit it: I set her against her husband. After being foolish enough to marry them, I tried to break them apart.

I had no idea how dangerous this might be until three weeks ago, when I received a phone call from Guadeloupe in the middle of the night. I was asleep, and I walked out into the hallway to get the phone because Father Remy is half deaf and he sleeps without his hearing aids. I recognized the voice immediately, but understood nothing. All I knew was that she was terribly upset. I tried to talk to her, to make some sense out of the sounds coming at me through the receiver, but it was like her confession: all sound, no meaning. I hated to let go of the phone, but finally I did, and then I struggled to get dressed and ran out to the car.

It was a long drive, more than twenty miles, but I goaded the old K-car up past its redline and crouched forward in anticipation as the farm lights whipped past me on either side like shooting stars. I concentrated on the road, connecting the stream of yellow dots that disappeared beneath the hood, and I tried with rank desperation to avoid thinking about what might be happening at that moment. I had no idea what Lucius might be capable of. I was responsible for everything. I swore that this time I was not going to quibble about legalities; I was going to take her away from there without any further hesitation.

When I turned off the highway onto their rutted laneway, I was almost afraid to go any further. Maybe I should call the police, I thought. But I had already decided, and this time I was going to force myself to go through with my decision. The car bounced along the shadowy road like a shopping cart on a motocross track, but I kept the accelerator down, and finally I crested the last hummock and came into view of their yard light. Guadeloupe was there, outside, leaning against one of the empty bird cages. She was unharmed as far as I could tell. I stopped the car and waited there for a second, wondering where Lucius and his dogs had gone. Then I got outside and walked toward her. She met me a few steps from the front door of the house, and stood between me and the building as if to stop me from seeing inside.

"He has going to hell," she said. She was backlit by the feeble kitchen light which shone through the screen door. I stood apart from her, trying to see her eyes. She had sounded so wild on the phone, yet she was almost serene now. I heard the κ-car's engine ticking as it cooled.

"Who?" I said. "The wolf, el lobo?"

"No," she said. "Him."

As she spoke I saw her eyes, and they were full of darkness like a deer's, and I stepped forward to embrace her, my fingers interlocked behind her waist as if in prayer. I felt her small breasts against me, and her legs through the thin cotton of her dress. She held me too, her forearms crossed behind my head, pulling my face down toward her shoulder. The smell of Lucius's cigarettes in her hair.

"You will forgive," she said.

It was an unmeasurable time, a time that would have a before and an after but no connection to either of them. The kitchen light diffracting through her hair like a comet. I couldn't speak. My legs began to shiver, not from cold. She was whispering again but I didn't register the words, only the general shapes of them. There had been a party. Adeline Lajeunesse and a man named Percy and another one. Cards. Moonshine. Something unpardonable.

"Imperdonable," she repeated more loudly. "He said to me things, he did to me things. Now he is in hell."

"What do you mean?" I said. I loosened my grip on her waist and tried to step back so I could look at her face, but she wouldn't let me. She held on tighter to my neck. I felt her rib cage pulsing like a bird's. Through her hair, in the dim space of the kitchen, I thought I saw something move.

"I hit him," she said, and finally loosened her arms from my neck. "With the gun. You will forgive?"

"You haven't – "

I broke away from her then, and ran toward the screen door. She didn't follow. I opened the door and stepped into the room, my shoes loud on the hollow floor. Lucius was laid on his back across the spindly table, his treadless yellow bootsoles facing me and the rest of him receding toward the far wall like a wide-angle photo. The boots, the curving planetary mound of his plaid belly, and in the far distance a spray of crazy bristles from his beard. Both arms were cast over the sides of the table in a gesture of irrelevance. His dozen dogs were crouched near his right hand like diffident apostles, unsure if they should lick the palm. They wore the badges of their own multiple wounds, their contusions and amputations and missing organs, but they hadn't considered that their healer might be vulnerable too. They glanced back and forth from Lucius to me, licking their black lips in consternation.

"Lord save us," I said, but I still didn't move. Three chrome chairs were overturned, and an old lever-action rifle was braced against one of them, the barrel pointing above the dogs' heads. The whole place smelled of disinfectant-grade moonshine. I heard the screen door swing open behind me and felt Guadeloupe standing there although she didn't touch me.

"He was a devil," she said.

I stepped toward the table, on the far side from the dogs, over the chair and the gun. My leg brushed against his hand, which was stiff. The head was leaned back on the arborite, the rimy mouth wide open as if awaiting a tonsil exam. The left eye was half open, so Lucius looked like one of his dogs, piratical and squinty. The wide white tract of his forehead was interrupted by a gargantuan knob that protruded above his right eyebrow like a nascent horn.

One of the dogs keened as I bent over to listen for breath at the toothy cavern of Lucius's mouth. I looked back down the body toward the metallic worn-through toes of the workboots and saw Guadeloupe framed between them, still holding the screen door open, watching almost nonchalantly. I've seen a lot of corpses in my time as a priest, and I knew without checking for a pulse that this was one. No sign of respiration. I could sense the frigid inertness of the body without even touching it.

"May the Lord Jesus Christ have mercy on your soul," I said, reflexively, and drew a sign of the cross in the air above his head. I couldn't help thinking about my own role in this. First marrying them, and then turning Guadeloupe against her husband. Coveting her. The magnitude of my sins rose up in my mind with dizzying force, a whirlwind of iniquity that engulfed me so suddenly I almost cowered down against the body. Guadeloupe's eyes, and the questioning eyes of the dogs, and the baleful Polyphemus on the table squinting up at me.

"Forgive me," I said, and placed my hands over Lucius's face, and closed my own eyes. But I didn't see darkness. I saw a vague misty nimbus surrounding an empty shape. It looked almost like the Horse Head Nebula, except this shape was a human form, head and shoulders ensconced in light. Lucius's pate was resinous and cold. The skin around his wound was so taut it seemed that some kind of volcanic excrescence was about to burst forth. The empty shape came closer. It waded through the light, down and down, toward a place behind my eyes. When it arrived there, I felt something hot and fugitive flooding down my arms and into Lucius's face.

I pulled my hands away and stepped back, kicking an empty

moonshine bottle with my heel. It spun like a lobbed hatchet or a throwing star, something deadly, ringing against the nailheads that protruded from the floorboards, and it stopped with the open screw-top pointing at me. I held my hands away from myself, palms up, like a scrubbed surgeon. I almost expected them to be stained, but they were as white and damp as ever. I glanced at Guadeloupe, who was staring behind me at the corpse, her eyes all pupil, her fingers clenched on the edge of the screen door. I was going to say something, but didn't. A sound interrupted me, a sound like the wings of crows in the distance, approaching in their black and shapeless cloak to smother my words. It grew louder for several seconds and then stopped abruptly with an almost flatulent burst, a hideous piglike snort cut off at the crescendo. I turned around involuntarily, despite my furious desire to keep staring at the screen door, and I focused on the body in time to see Lucius swimming his maddened way into a sitting position. Guadeloupe said something in Spanish. Lucius edged forward on the table until his feet swung freely. He took another breath, shook his head three times, and then he recognized his wife. He gazed at her with idiotic adoration.

"The Lord is with thee," he said, and smiled childishly, his eyes suddenly gushing with tears. At the sound of his voice the dogs broke into thunderous exultation, and they all sprang toward his lap with slavering jowls and frantically wagging tails. It looked like he would be torn apart, but he fended off the horde with quick thrusts of his feet and blithe breast-stroke motions of his hands. The smaller dogs caromed away like deflected hockey pucks and tumbled to the bottom of the pile. The larger ones recoiled back onto their haunches, howled, and jumped again. Lucius kept pace with them, his limbs pumping rhythmically as if he was trapped in a crazy new-fangled exercycle. But he didn't speak to the dogs or give them any sign of recognition; his eyes were all for Guadeloupe, and he aimed that blissful smile at her as if bestowing a gift or benediction, his copious tears dangling from his beard like jewelry.

Guadeloupe had been standing motionless with one hand on the screen door, but suddenly it slammed shut and I glimpsed a swirl of her dress as she fled toward the river. I burst out the door after her, leaving Lucius to contend with the dogs. There was a rectangle of light on the wet grass and after that only murky half-tones and the shocking face of the moon and the blur of movement that had to be Guadeloupe. She was faster than I would have believed. I dodged a birdcage, a sapling, a prehistoric tractor. My feet seemed to make no sound, and the howl of the dogs quickly receded. I lost Guadeloupe in a stand of trees and slowed down to get my bearings. In a few steps I saw the river below me, a fan of moonlight on the rippled water. I stopped, listened for something other than the quick flow of my own breathing and the muted din of the dogs. Nothing.

"Guadeloupe?" I called. "It's only me. Father Silvan. Don't be afraid."

She didn't answer, though I knew she had to be close enough to hear. My eyes had adjusted to the dark and I could see that there were only about twenty trees in the bluff. If she had run across to the next clump of poplars I would have seen her in the moonlight.

"Come with me in the car," I said. "I can take you to a safe place, a place where you won't be afraid. You shouldn't stay here anymore."

I saw a quick movement from behind one of the poplar trees near the edge of the river bank, and I was just beginning to smile when the moon made a sudden swoop in the sky, down to the water and back up, and I heard a noise like an apple dropped on cement. Something had struck my head. A rock. It tumbled to the ground at my feet.

"Go!" Guadeloupe hissed. Another rock bounced off the tree I was leaning on. "You are my bad dream. The wolf. It is you!"

I shrank behind the tree, pressing my shoulder against it and standing as straight as possible to minimize the angle. I bleated her name but she didn't answer. My skull was throbbing above my right ear where the rock had hit, and I reached up to check for blood. I felt a dampness on my scalp, and the beginnings of a lump, but it didn't seem serious. I heard Guadeloupe moving again in the bush, probably gathering more rocks.

"I'm trying to help you," I pleaded.

She appeared suddenly beside me, brandishing a huge

leafy stick the size of an uprooted sapling. Her face was out-lined in the moonlight, her once-demure features clenched in grim ferocity.

"Only a devil could do what you have done," she said.

I had been preparing to reason with her, to negotiate, but now I hesitated. Her certainty unnerved me. What *had* I done? That empty shape was still lurking inside me somewhere. I could feel it prowling in my body like a piranha in a bowl.

"I didn't –" I said, but I couldn't complete my denial. To say anything more about it would be to give it a life of its own.

"You did," she said, and pushed the sapling toward me, shaking a cluster of foliage in my face. I tried to wrench it away from her but ended up with only a handful of leaves.

"Devil!" she yelled.

Our scuffle was interrupted by the sound of Lucius calling Guadeloupe's name. He said it as if he had never pronounced it before, which may well have been the case. He had always called her Lou until now. Guadeloupe and I turned toward the house to see his colossal silhouette crowded into the doorway, a clamour of dogs behind him. He peered back and forth across the yard and repeated her name again like a bird call.

Guadeloupe took a quick breath as if she was going to answer him, but before she could speak the dogs made a con-centrated rush at Lucius and pushed him out into the yard. They flowed around him as he stumbled in the grass, and when he stopped they kept running toward Guadeloupe and me, moving as a single being, a dozen-headed mongrel Cerberus that stretched out into a serpent as the larger dogs pulled into the lead. Even though each of them was missing something, they all had their jaws and most of them still had teeth, which were visible in the moonlight as they barked and growled and bayed across the yard. Lucius ran behind them, waving his arms and trying unsuccessfully to whistle while hyperventilating.

"Hurry!" I said, and I grabbed the sapling again and tried to drag Guadeloupe toward the car. She followed for several steps, but then she let go and I was catapulted toward the stream of dogs, stumbling nose-first over the quackgrass with a severed piece of poplar dragging behind me like a travois.

"I hope they kill you," she yelled.

I didn't have time to plead with her again – the lop-eared doberman was nearly upon me, and I swung the sapling around to defend myself. I was still twenty yards from the car. The dog bounded straight for the end of the stick, clamped its jaws onto it, and flailed its head around like a frenzied shark. The sound was horrible. Two other dogs caught up with the doberman and snapped at the stick. It would only be a second before they figured out that I wasn't connected to it. I had a momentary vision of my own leg caught in such a hopeless tug-of-war, my foot swinging back and forth like a kite in a tornado. I dropped the sapling and fled.

The large dogs stayed with the stick, but the second wave

– those with short or missing legs – saw me making my escape, and they raced across the yard to intercept me. Five steps from the car I tripped on a kamikaze terrier and only regained my balance when I banged into the passenger door. I yanked on the handle and wedged myself in, but as I did I was savaged by a three-legged beagle that clenched onto my right ankle and wouldn't let go, as if the mutt believed it had found its own lost leg and refused to relinquish it a second time. I had to reach down and pry the dog's mouth open, risking further injury from the flurry of snapping jaws that surrounded the beagle. I succeeded, and shut the door quickly, and slid across the seat to the driver's side. Lucius and Guadeloupe were no longer visible, even when I switched on the headlights. Nothing but dogs and empty cages in the yard. Maybe I should have waited, but my ankle was bleeding and my forehead ached and I couldn't even begin to think about what had happened. I started the car and spun out of the yard, mulching two long strips of grass behind me. I kept looking in the rear-view mirror for Guadeloupe, but she was gone. I haven't seen her since.

That's how I remember it, but I can't even trust my memory when I try to decide what happened between me and Lucius Drake. I only know that something *did* happen. He was dead, and then he was alive. I wish I could say otherwise – that he was never dead in the first place and all I did was revive him. That would reassure Guadeloupe that I'm not a devil, and it would put to rest all of Lucius's rumours about my supposedly saintly activities.

Or maybe it wouldn't. These days people seem more willing than ever to believe whatever wild tales and tabloid miracles that certain unscrupulous people proclaim as gospel truth. I have given homilies on this subject over the years, warning my parishioners against the hazards of misplaced faith, but it doesn't seem to have done any good. Probably half of them are taking part in Lucius's Novena right now, praising me as a healer.

I would have thought that in our sceptical age an oversupply of belief would be the last of our problems. But now I see that belief is everywhere. It has been suppressed for too long, and it springs out from people's souls before they even know it, latching onto whatever sensational legends are near at hand.

Which brings me to a question I can't ask anyone. Why, in this new age of conviction, can I not find any for myself?

FRIDAY, JUNE 17
ST. JOSEPH'S ABBEY

I have been up all night recounting my sins, and a few minutes ago the bell for matins rang with hammered purity, as if the great rusty clapper was fixed at the base of my skull. It was an apocalyptic tolling of my unabsolved transgressions, and I knew, by the end of it, that Father Remy and I may well be each other's damnation.

Did we come to hate each other at the same time, or was one of us first off the mark? It was a long time ago. I know that the smell of him has always offended me most. The sweet corruption of his wine, the insidious stench of his taxidermical experiments. For years now when I've celebrated mass I have gagged on the Blood of Christ because it reminds me of Remy's breath. And even if his stuffed animals didn't stink I would still hate them. I can't go anywhere in the rectory without a crowd of glass-eyed creatures watching me. That enormous pike in the bathroom, the stupid partridge peering down from the top of the fridge. For eleven years I have lived in a menagerie of corpses.

I despise him, but I refuse to seek absolution for it. There are other sins on my conscience too, unforgiven because unconfessed. For a long time I have kept my gravest sins to myself because I couldn't stand to recount my weaknesses to Remy in the confessional. And since I know his own shortcomings better than he knows them himself, I've noticed that he is similarly reluctant to confess. There is the matter of his precious sacramental wine, for example. He orders ten times as much as any other parish, yet he has never confessed that most of it funnels down his gullet during his daily "meditations." He is an intemperate man, a glutton, a drunk. And he's done something far worse than all this, I know he has, though I can't prove it. He's taken her away. Separated us. I could have forgiven him for everything else, but for that – may he die with the stain on his soul.

I didn't suspect him at the time. My thoughts were too consumed with the image of Lucius Drake rising from the dead, sitting up on his kitchen table like a hill-billy Frankenstein, calling out to his wife with a terrifying sincerity in his eyes. I told Remy I had the flu, but it was really a delirium of nightmares. A dark human shape slid out of my dreams like smoke and danced with malicious glee on the ceiling. Whenever I wasn't looking, it came back down and pounded me onto the bed. In my lucid moments, I wondered if the dog that had bitten me was rabid. But I didn't tell Remy about the dog bite because I knew he would take me to the hospital, and then I would miss my Saturday evening appointment with Guadeloupe. More than anything I needed to hear her voice and see the dusky outline of her face on the other side of the confessional grate. The thought that I would see her was the only thing that kept me from surrendering to my hallucinations.

By Saturday afternoon I was able to drag myself out of bed, and I pretended to be fully recovered. But Remy told me I shouldn't celebrate mass because it would only make me sick again, and because I might infect half the congregation through the vector of the Holy Eucharist. He thought I was liable to commit a heresy in my condition, to drop the host or garble the words of transubstantiation or take the Lord's name in vain during the homily. It surprised him when I pushed him aside and stumbled down the hall toward the sacristy. When he didn't follow, I thought it meant I had won. Now I see that it only made him change his plans.

He must have done it while I was waiting in the sacristy, peering out into the church every thirty seconds in the hope that Guadeloupe would be there. I delayed the beginning of Mass for ten minutes. Members of the congregation sensed that something was wrong; they glanced wincingly at her empty pew and then looked away, as if an indispensable part of their churchly ritual had been a view of her braided black hair silhouetted against the pulpit. I retreated to the sacristy time after time, hoping that Lucius had had a flat tire or had been too drunk to maintain his perfect record for punctuality. At ten after seven I looked out again. The pew was still vacant, but Sister Sophie had moved to the row behind it and she was kneeling there, glaring at me with her lips clamped shut as if to deny the possibility of orifices. I had no choice but to begin.

I said mass in disjointed double-time, wanting to get it over with before I lost consciousness. The altar servers could hardly keep up with me. They scrambled back and forth from the altar, jiggling the cruets, and they rang the bells several minutes too late. I remember I gave an impromtu homily on miracles, arguing that they don't happen anymore. The congregation – all except Sister Sophie – accepted this with their usual vacant placidity. I tried to skip the recessional hymn, but they sang it out of habit, so I had to limp around the priestly circuit with the Bible held on high, dragging my dog-bitten foot like a ball and chain. At the end, I collapsed in Guadeloupe's pew and sat there while the parishioners filed out, and then I handed the Bible off to one of the altar servers.

After a minute of rest, I made my way back to the confessional and enthroned myself there. It smelled of Remy: *Chateau Quatorze Rouge* and embalming fluid. I waited there for Guadeloupe's voice to come to me out of the dark. But instead there were only the furtive murmurings of the usual old ladies, who recited their lists of peccadilloes and their acts of contrition with grim succinctness, as if they were afraid of wasting God's time. Mrs. Allen had been squabbling with her neighbour again, over some mythical transgression involving a garden hose and a lawn mower. Sister Sophie complained as always that she hadn't harangued enough people into performing good works. Mrs. Boulieu was still gaining weight. I pronounced the absolutions mechanically, letting the ritual carry on without me, still hoping, after each harridan was absolved, that Guadeloupe would step into the cubicle and announce by her presence that everything had been set right again.

It didn't happen. There were only more of the same dull-witted sinners. Before my ordination I had looked forward to the intimacy of the confessional, the direct connection between the penitent and God, with myself as the intermediary. But ninety-nine percent of the time it wasn't as dramatic or as satisfying as I had imagined. Mostly it was just a curdled miasma of fetid breath and fear. Sometimes I think my Uncle William was right, years ago, when he nicknamed his outhouse "The Confessional." There are many similarities. The closeted design, the roughshod wooden construction, the single hole through which the business is conducted. People go into both places to expose themselves, to deposit their vilest productions and then walk out, relieved of a burden. It's fine unless you happen to be the priest, sitting at the other end of the hole, bombarded with iniquities.

Guadeloupe was different. She was one of the beautiful confessors, the ones who remind you that this is a sacrament, a connection to God. With her, every confession was a sonata of grief and supplication, a tremulous prayer that could break your heart even if you didn't understand a word. When I absolved her at the end of each performance, I always felt like I was the one who had been blessed.

Now, when the last of the old ladies had said their share, and I had to admit that Guadeloupe wasn't coming, the first thing I felt was the loss of that exquisite experience. I mourned for it. I sat in the musty dark and remembered the incomprehensible confidences we had shared. I wondered if I would have the opportunity again. She had forsaken me this time.

It was only after a long session of despondent self-pity that I arrived at the notion that Guadeloupe might not have *chosen* to miss our weekly meeting. It was a dizzying thought, so much more terrifying because it was the only sensible explanation. Of course. She would never willingly have missed her confession. If she wasn't there, it meant that someone had prevented her.

I gagged at the inexorability of that logic, and at my own stupidity in not seeing it earlier. After what she had done to Lucius on Wednesday night, it only made sense that he would have retaliated.

Much as I never wanted to see Lucius Drake's face again, I lurched out of the confessional and scrambled around the back of the rectory to the K-car. I drove, as I had the last time, in a fury of blue smoke and unflagging momentum, the old Reliant wailing like a clogged vacuum cleaner as I tromped mercilessly on the throttle. Delirium swarmed over me when I reached the outskirts of town, and all I remember of the rest of the trip is that plaintive sound of the engine. When I pulled into Lucius's yard I started to regain my senses. I stopped near the river bank and put the engine to rest. There was no sign of anyone. The sun was hanging just above the horizon, suspended in the branches of some worm-infested poplars. I rolled down the window and listened for the dogs or some other sign of life. The wind off the river sounded in the trees like a waterfall, but there was nothing else. I studied the house. It was the first time I had seen it in daylight. A basementless two-room hovel with unpainted chipboard siding that had aged into a mosaic of grey tones. On the south side, the sun had curled pieces of the chipboard so badly that they wagged in the breeze like leaves. Lucius didn't believe in paint, except in the case of his half-ton, which he smeared with flat-black Tremclad whenever the rust started getting out of hand.

The rest of the buildings leaned against poplar trees in a haphazard semicircle behind the house: three ash-coloured granaries with tufts of wheat and barley growing out of the shingles, a sway-backed workshop supporting a ponderous rack of moose antlers above the doorless entrance, and the skeleton of a miniature barn which had been started at least a decade earlier and never completed. All of these structures were mounted on skids, as if for ease of relocation. Scattered around them were carcasses of automobiles with their hoods and doors wide open, saplings protruding from the engine compartments. The empty bird cages were there too, all of them hopelessly overgrown with sprouted birdseed except the biggest one, which contained a dozen of Guadeloupe's dog-wary chickens. The poor woman didn't stand a chance in that environment. No matter how hard she worked, she would never catch up with Lucius's decades of neglect.

I got out of the car, still scanning the yard for any sign of the dogs. Remy's diamond-willow cane was in the back seat, and I reached in to get it, even though I knew it would be nearly useless against those ravening hounds. I walked up to the house and peered in the screen door. No lights on, no sounds except for the wind. I called Guadeloupe's name, in a whisper at first and then a little louder. The door looked directly into the kitchen, which seemed unchanged from Wednesday night. Guadeloupe would never have left her kitchen in such a state. There were empty tumblers on the floor beside the washstand, and three glazed crocks of moonshine against the far wall, and an array of playing cards spread across the arborite table where Lucius had been laid out. The gun was the only thing missing.

I turned away from the screen door and walked down to the river bank. A hundred yards downstream a dead cow was floating in the water, two legs jutting skyward, her belly swollen like a nightmare pregnancy. She was hung up on the pilings of the old bridge, which protruded above the high water mark and had collected so much debris over the years that it looked like a beaver dam. I had gone fishing at that spot with Abe Nickolichuk just after I'd arrived in Windfall. That was how I first heard the legends about Lucius Drake. Nobody fished there anymore, either because people were nervous about stumbling onto Lucius's not-so-secret moonshine operation or because the pickerel had stopped coming. Either way, everyone blamed Lucius. Some people said he had stretched a net across the river every night until there were no fish left.

I knew I should walk downstream along the bank, but I was too afraid of what I might find. I remembered Guadeloupe's dreams about the river and the black wolf. The sun was beginning to set, and already the waning moon was rising out of the trees on the far side of the bank. It was time to leave the searching to the police. There were things I didn't want them to know about, for Guadeloupe's sake more than my own, but I couldn't keep them out of this any longer. I should have told them long ago, I thought. Maybe they would have taken her away and given her a chance at a better life.

I started back toward the car, but before I got there I heard something from behind the house, a droning sound like a swarm of bees lost in the wind. The sound wavered and then disappeared in a gust that brought a surge of applause from the trees. I walked around the house, moving carefully among the tufts of long grass, trying to avoid the hidden car parts and rotting boards that were lost in the vegetation. The yard was encompassed in shadow. I heard the noise again when I got behind the house, and I followed it past the ghostly frame of the barn and into the woods. I couldn't find a trail, but the trees were large enough that there was little undergrowth. Fifty yards past the barn I saw a clearing, so I headed for it, moving as quietly as possible and stopping every few seconds to listen. The sound came again, and I recognized that it was a voice. Lucius's voice, I thought, but it had a high wavering pitch that seemed unlike his usual gruff monotone. As if he was pleading with someone.

I stepped up onto a fallen log and squinted through the pattern of tree trunks and branches into the clearing, where I saw the unmistakable shape of Lucius's truck. It was parked on a little hummock about twenty yards into the field, its gaping toothless grille and bulbous headlights facing down toward me. I walked up the fallen log, balancing with arms outspread as if poised for flight, swinging the willow cane as a counterbalance. When I got near the stump I reached out to a sapling to hold myself still. The voice continued its halting soliloquy. Through an opening in the branches I made out the head and shoulders of a large and woolly man standing in the truck box, facing away. This could only have been Lucius, Samson-haired and mountainous, regaling someone with stories of his latest crimes. Maybe he was confessing what he had done with Guadeloupe.

I waited there for several seconds, hoping to see something else or to distinguish a few incriminating words, but it didn't work. My sore ankle ached from balancing on the log, so I stepped down, crunching a hidden twig. A dog yipped briefly from somewhere on the far side of the truck, but Lucius scolded it and it was quiet again. My hands were trembling. I was afraid of him at that moment, and even more frightened of the dogs, but I couldn't leave now without finding out what had happened to Guadeloupe. I would not allow myself to turn away as I had done so many times before.

It was the last point of evening, when every second seems to bring a palpable encroachment of darkness. I had to hurry if I wanted to see anything. I walked along another fallen log, then crossed over to a patch of moss. I circled the clearing, staying as far as possible out of the dogs' range of hearing. When I got far enough to the west I turned back toward Lucius, who was still speaking in that eerie falsetto. From this position I had a side view of the truck, which should have enabled me to see who Lucius was talking to. But I still couldn't see anyone else. I crept closer and listened. It seemed so familiar, each sound arriving on the edge of my expectation, as if I was the one who was speaking.

Then in the midst of my straining to understand, one word became clear: "Christ." I held my breath to listen even harder, imagining Lucius to be chanting a great curse against his enemies. The word came again, and then once more a few seconds later. And suddenly the chant took shape around that word, like a kaleidoscope image resolving itself into a picture. I knew these words so well that I understood them even before Lucius spoke them.

"If for this life only we have hoped in Christ, we are of all people most to be pitied. But in fact Christ has been raised from the dead, the first fruits of those who have died. For since death came through a human being, the resurrection of the dead has also come through a human being; for as all die in Adam, so all will be made alive in Christ."

Lucius kept reading in his plodding style, and I heard the words of the Apostle echo in my mind as I trudged quickly through the bush, not bothering to push aside the branches that raked across my face and pulled at my hair. I stopped at the edge of the clearing. The dogs, all twelve of them, were hunched on the ground behind the truck, and Lucius was standing on the tailgate holding the Bible up to the waning light, reading unperturbed although each member of his audience was glaring at me. I didn't move. Lucius's beard wagged with each syllable he pronounced. I recognized his Bible – the red leather cover with a brass zipper that dangled from the spine like a fish hook. It was the one I had given Guadeloupe.

"The last enemy to be destroyed," Lucius said, "is death."

At this, I stepped forward, and one of the dogs keened. I halted again, looking at the wolflike eyes of the hounds, their twelve muzzles curling upward like burning paper.

Lucius stopped reading and turned slowly around with the Bible still open in front of him.

"What have you done?" I shouted. "Where is she?"

Lucius didn't answer for a long time. His wiry black hair wavered in the breeze like flames, and his eyes seemed to be focused on something in the distance behind me. The Bible quaked in his hands.

"Father!" he said.

He closed the Bible carefully and then stepped down from the tailgate and shambled toward me with his arms held open, the red book dangling from his right hand. The dogs followed at his heels. He was wearing the same clothes as Wednesday night, the plaid Flannelite shirt half-unbuttoned, the grease-stained jeans, the work boots abraded through to the gleaming steel toes. He moved stiffly, as though his limbs were reluctant to obey. Suddenly I thought he was going to grab me, and I brandished the walking stick to keep him back. He was surprised at this; he stopped about ten feet from me, his arms held out like a scarecrow, his whole face exuding bovine earnestness. Apparently he hadn't intended to do me any harm, but still I kept the stick raised above my head for several seconds, to let him know I was serious. He didn't move. I noticed that there wasn't a bump or even a bruise on his forehead where Guadeloupe had hit him.

"Where is your wife?" I said.

Lucius lowered his arms and held the Bible in both mottled hands. The skin on his arms and neck had been scalded years ago in an accident at his still. The hair in his beard grew in crazy swirls because of it.

"She's gone, Father," he said. "She left just after you, and I've been praying ever since. The way I learned from her. She was teaching me all the time, even though I didn't know it. She showed me the Novena, the nine day prayer, she did one of those after the wedding. Every day out in the field with her prayer book, Spanish coming out of her like a whirlwind. I didn't know I was learning anything by it at the time. But I was."

He held up the stolen Bible as if to prove what he had learned. I didn't know what to say. I looked at this huge man before me, this reprobate who was known far and wide for his drinking and gambling and violence. This man who had made a career out of hatefulness. Standing there now with a Bible in his hands and piety leaking out his eyes.

"You've done something with her," I said. "You can't hide it."

Lucius looked down at the Bible and spoke to it quietly. "No Father. *She* did something to *me*. And you did. You know. When I woke up – when you brought me back – I knew Guadeloupe wasn't my wife. She was an angel, sent to change me. Just like you."

I remembered the feel of Lucius's forehead against my fingertips: the coldness of the skin, the latex pliability of it, except above the left eyebrow where a monumental purple mound was jutting like a freakish geological formation. It was the feel of a corpse.

"I didn't –" I began, but I lost track of what I was going to say. Lucius took three steps toward me.

"You brought me back," he said, nodding slowly. "Guadeloupe saw it too. The Lord was working through your hands."

He motioned with the Bible toward the truck, as if inviting me to join in with the canine audience. I didn't respond. I had no idea what to do.

"I'm praying a Novena of Novenas," Lucius went on. "Nine times nine! Eighty-one days of thanks to the Lord, for bringing me back from the dark, for giving me the chance to make up for what I was. For showing me the truth!"

"You're not even Catholic," I said.

He only shrugged. "You're the one that saved me."

I sensed movement to my left, and I glanced over to see a one-eyed pug creeping toward me on its belly, a porcine tale wagging pathetically behind. The dogs had closed in on Lucius and were now beginning to encircle me too. Not menacingly but gregariously, as if they were welcoming me into their pack. An earless rotweiler and the insane three-legged beagle that had so recently tasted my flesh were approaching from the other side. The thought that they were accepting me was somehow more frightening than if they had attacked. I backed away toward the edge of the bush.

"Keep them off," I said. Lucius didn't move, but the dogs stopped in any case.

"I'm a changed man," Lucius pleaded.

"Well, I'm not," I said. "I want to know what happened to Guadeloupe, and if you won't tell me I'll have to go to the police."

I waited for an answer, but Lucius stood there silently with the Bible held out like a biscuit. His eyes displayed the sadness of a martyr. It was a very Catholic expression. But it didn't change the fact that Lucius Drake was a manipulator and a blasphemer and possibly much worse.

"I'm telling them she's missing," I said. "I pray to God she's safe."

I turned and thrashed my way through a clump of wild roses before I reached the dark cover of the trees. Lucius was speaking again, but I couldn't understand him. I blundered through the woods, sidestepping the looming poplar trunks, half-tripping on invisible fallen logs. Occasionally the moon appeared above the canopy, and I aimed for it. I reached the unfinished barn and found a path there which led out into the yard. A thin layer of fog had come up from the river, and it lay over the hood of the car like a snowbank.

As I crossed the yard I heard Lucius's voice calling insistently, and the sudden baying of dogs. I bolted toward the car, dragging my injured ankle. When I got in I locked the door behind myself and started the engine. In the headlights I saw nothing but fog, but I floored the accelerator anyway, and cranked the wheel sharply to the left. The rear bumper caught on one of the old bird cages and uprooted it. There was a screech of chicken wire against the K-car's paint, then a red tumbleweed shape in the rear-view mirror. Lucius's house sprang into the headlights and I swerved, the front tires sliding into the rutted path just in time to jerk the car out of a collision course and direct it toward the highway.

I drove so recklessly on the way back to town that I could have killed myself. I would have done it too – turned off the road into a poplar bluff or simply opened my door and tumbled out onto the asphalt at ninety miles an hour – except I knew I had to get to the RCMP. If there was any possibility that Guadeloupe was still alive, I had to give them every chance of finding her, and if she was not alive I wanted to be sure that Lucius was brought to justice.

I was so overfull of frightening knowledge that it came spilling out of me in breathless gouts as soon as I stepped in the door of the police station. But the officer at the desk interrupted me before I got to the important parts. She sat me down on a vinyl bench in the lobby and gave me a paper cone full of rusty-tasting water and said there was no need to worry. I got the feeling that she had been expecting me. She said the police knew where Guadeloupe was, and that she was safe, and that she would get in touch with me by phone if she wanted to. I didn't think I had even mentioned her name yet. When I asked if I could see her, the officer said her location was classified information.

I drank the last of the water and gave the paper cone back to the officer, who smiled uncertainly. I was overwhelmed, first with relief that Guadeloupe was safe, and then with a violent sense of emptiness. The image of her vacant pew flickered in my mind. She really had forsaken me. In her time of need, she had sought the help of strangers rather than turning to her only friend.

The officer left me there in the lobby and went back to the mound of papers on her desk. She didn't look at me again. She chewed the end of a pencil and rifled through sheaves of pink forms, trying to suppress a bemused half-smile that indicated she had all the information I wanted. If she had been one of my parishioners maybe I would have tried to wheedle it out of her, but she had the look of a Pentecostal about her so I knew I didn't have a chance. I stood up unsteadily and hobbled to the heavy glass doors, which opened soundlessly onto the night.

As I drove home I was surprisingly lucid, but I could sense that the black shape of my nightmares was girding itself for another assault on my psyche. I resolved not to let myself fall asleep, though I knew even as I made the resolution that it was pointless. By the time I got to the rectory I was already on the edge of collapse, and the lurid dreams were swarming in my mind like bingo balls in a machine. All I wanted to do was flop down on my bed and let the dark shape have its way with me.

But as I stumbled down the stairs I heard a voice calling me from the library. It was Remy. I should have known. I leaned against the door and peered inside. He was ensconced in his leatherette recliner as usual, suturing a furred piece of road kill back into some semblance of a living animal. I recognized this one as the red squirrel he had run over on the way to the nursing home a couple of weeks earlier. I remembered how overjoyed he had been at the lucky happenstance of that accident, waltzing into the kitchen before supper with his prize held up by the tail. I've often wondered why a far higher than average number of creatures have met their deaths beneath the wheels of our pastoral K-car, and always when he is driving. At his confession a few days after the squirrel's demise I had tried to get him to admit that it had not been entirely accidental. *Any other sins to confess? No? Nothing else you feel remorseful about? All right then. For your penance, recite "All Creatures Great and Small" ten times.* Even in the context of the Blessed Sacrament, he had refused to acknowledge his guilt. Since then, I had been wondering when to expect his revenge, and now when I saw the tell-tale arching of his winglike eyebrows, I knew the time had arrived.

"Where have you been, in your condition?" he asked, still looking down at the squirrel which he cradled in his left arm, Madonna-and-Child fashion, while jabbing a curved needle into its overstuffed belly.

"At the nursing home," I said. "Checking in on Mrs. Frenette."

He knew I was lying. He shook his head slowly, still gazing at the squirrel through his bifocals.

"You'll have to put all that behind you," he said. "Chasing around. Not good for your health."

He looked up at me, grinning smugly, and then he used his wrist to push his glasses further up on his nose. I couldn't speak. I was wrenched by a sudden recognition, and it felt like my entrails were draining out of me into some unquenchable void. I knew that smile. It was the same one I had just seen at the police station.

Yes. Remy had more information, and he wanted me to beg for it. I nearly did. I almost got down on my knees and prayed at the hem of his garment for whatever bits of knowledge he might care to fling away – but my pride prevented me. I figured it out in any case. I had been chasing the wrong person. In my frenzy to question Lucius, it had never occurred to me that anyone else might try to take Guadeloupe away. And Remy, of all people! I remembered the times he had shot covetous looks at Guadeloupe and me when we were doing our English lessons in the kitchen.

We waited for each other to speak, Remy with his hands moving obscenely over the squirrel's abdomen, me quaking under the wall-eyed gaze of the balding mule deer above the mantel. Death, everywhere. I remember a sudden profusion of sweat beneath my clothes and a simultaneous heaviness and buoyancy in my limbs and the crazy eyes of that dead deer staring me down. Remy knows the rest better than I. He must have seen me slide to the floor, and then maybe he smiled to himself again, or maybe he made the sign of the cross and asked God for pardon. Either way he kept it a secret. He dragged me to my room and somehow pried me up onto the bed and then he abandoned me there in my sweat-soaked clothes. I slept right through to morning without a single dream.

SUNDAY JUNE 19
ST. JOSEPH'S ABBEY

I've been remembering the fall of 1961, when my grandmother was dying and my Uncle William came to stay with us in Saskatoon. He hated the hospital, so he rarely visited Grandma, even though she was the reason he'd gotten time off from his job at the saw mill. He had lived for years in a log cabin near the Browneye reserve, and everything about the city intimidated him. For most of his visit he stayed in the house and played cribbage against himself, or listened to records on the RCA my father had bought that year. When I got home from school it was my job to keep him entertained, because my mother was always at the hospital.

I had only seen Grandma a few times myself since she had disappeared into the ambulance early one morning. The whole process of her degeneration frightened me so much that I tried to avoid the hospital too. She was partly paralysed. She spoke with difficulty and could only hold her rosary with one hand, which was a definite problem because she used it constantly, her fingers moving covertly beneath the hillock of blankets. I believed she was using the rosary as an abacus, counting and counting until she found the right number, the number of the saints marching in, the combination to the pearly gates. She told those prayer-worn beads with such furious determination that I knew she was near the end. It was almost a race, to see if she could reach that perfect number before her imperfect body failed her.

Uncle William and I could stay away because we had each other for an excuse. We never spoke about her when we were together, either because we were both genuinely terrified of her or because it was simply too awkward to speak of such things when we were busy killing animals. Which is what we did most of the time. We hunted together.

The first time we went was three days after Uncle William had arrived. I got home from school and found him waiting for me in the driveway, leaning against the fender of his mud-caked Buick. There were two shotguns in the back seat. He told me the government had set a bounty on crows, five cents for every pair of feet. He said I could keep the sixteen-gauge if I could shoot twenty dollars worth.

We drove south of town, close to the river valley where there was a good combination of tree cover and freshly cut wheat in the fields. He told me the birds always fed on the unharvested sheaves during the day and came back to the trees to roost in late afternoon. We parked on the edge of a muddy road allowance and then trudged into a clump of poplars and waited. We stood fifty feet apart, our pockets weighed down with shells.

After about half an hour of standing there without any sign, William pointed to the south, where the birds were coming in a huge cluster, moving with its own amorphous energy. The sound of their arrival was like an enormous threshing machine. I had to force myself not to start shooting until they had landed in the branches above me. I waited another second, then looked over to William. He gave the nod. We raised our guns simultaneously, and I shot without aiming. There was no need to aim. The birds lifted suddenly into the sky like pellets from my gun, and some of them fell down, and others landed quickly again, and others swarmed above me in disarray. I broke open my gun and dropped in another shell and fired again. William had a seven-shot magazine, and he was shooting like a gattling gun, rhythmically, with a long pause for reloading. After each shot it became harder to hit the birds because they wouldn't keep still. More and more I had to aim, and I wasn't good at it. I blasted at a column of them still swirling above the trees, but it was impossible to lead them because they were turning so quickly. I broke the gun open again and the empty shell popped over my shoulder. The smell of the powder was like the taste of pennies. I waited there with the gun still open, cradled in my arms with the barrel pointing down toward a dead crow lying near my feet. William was still firing, and I felt a shower of stray pellets coming back down, a couple of them bouncing off the brim of my hat. The sound of the birds was gone now, and was replaced by the tuning fork noise of aftershock in my skull.

William stopped shooting and turned to look at me.

"How many?" he yelled.

"Six or seven," I said, though I could only see four in the grass. I was sure I had seen more of them falling.

"I bet I got over thirty," William said. "There's probably two bucks worth here." He leaned his gun against a tree and reached for a bird, which dangled loose-necked from his large hand. Then he pulled a hunting knife out of his belt and jerked it against the crow, so its body fell back to the ground. He stuck the twiglike legs in his pocket and reached quickly for another bird.

I did the same, but my jacknife was so dull I had to saw at the crow's legs for several seconds. Its head wobbled, and the wings came open as if it would fly away upside-down. Everything about it was black, so black it looked blue in the sunlight, and its eyes were still open and the body still warm when it brushed against my hand. There was no sign of a wound on it. Finally my blade broke through one bone and then the other, and the body fluttered down between my boots. There was no blood on the legs, only white circles of hollow bone, and the feet were clenched as if palsied.

The shooting was always exciting, the wild rush and chaos of the birds wheeling above me, and the feel of the gun recoiling against my shoulder, and the nitric smell of explosions. Gathering the legs afterward made me feel sick at first, but after the second evening I came to see it as part of the hunt, and I began to reach for downed birds with the same quick enthusiasm as William did. It became easier after I sharpened my knife.

I had killed over three hundred birds when my grandmother died. They had brought her home two days earlier, and our hunting expeditions had been suspended. Most of the time we sat in the living room, just waiting for it to happen. Everyone was quiet. It was even too sombre to play a record. There were plenty of cakes and cookies that the neighbours had brought, but it was hard to enjoy them. All I could think was, please let me not see her again. I wanted to remember her differently. But my mother guilted me into it. That's how it happened that her last words were addressed to me.

Mom and William and I were in the room. Dad had gone to check on something at work, even though he had taken the week off. The priest had just left. It was dark in the room, and there were so many blankets on the bed that I thought she might not be there at all. I was just going to have a peek, a solemn moment, holding my breath, and then step back out – but Mom led me toward the bed and held me there by the shoulders. Grandma was awake. Her hand emerged from the edge of the blanket, trailing a loop of obsidian beads, and she gripped my forearm with a shocking strength. I remembered the shrivelled feet of the crows.

"Silvan," she said. "You are marked for God."

By the time the funeral was over, I had decided to become a priest.

I see now that I have always acquired my faith at second hand. I've needed someone to show me how and what to believe before I could do it for myself. Spiritual guidance, the Church calls it. I've even been a spiritual guide for others, passing on the same advice my counsellors had given to me. Sometimes I wonder if my counsellors did the same thing – if this spiritual guidance is nothing but an exalted rumour that circulates among us, without anyone knowing its source or its object.

But here at the abbey I can't obtain spiritual guidance in any case, even if I thought I could still believe in it. I must remain invisible, as the Bishop said. I can't even take the sacraments because I don't want to risk being recognized. I have enough trouble remaining inconspicuous at mealtimes here, without also exposing my face to the whole community in the chapel. So I must go without absolution, even as my sins seem to multiply with every examination of my conscience.

After Guadeloupe disappeared I felt a similar destitution. I needed someone else who would help me understand what I had done to Lucius. I already knew what Lucius himself thought, and I didn't want to ask him about it again. It seemed that I had no other options, since he and Guadeloupe were the only witnesses. But then I remembered: Guadeloupe had told me that Adeline Lajeunesse had been there earlier in the evening, at the party where all the trouble began.

I knew Adeline, or at least I had seen her a few times, walking along the river when I was delivering communion to the shut-ins on the reserve. Sometimes she called out to me, said embarrassing things that made me turn away, clutching my briefcase as if to shelter the consecrated hosts from her blasphemies. I remember her laugh. It was like the whine of an engine that won't quite start. She loved to laugh at me; she seemed to think my collar made me a perfect target for dirty jokes. One time she turned around and slid her spandex leggings down to her thighs, displaying the black lace of her panties and the two satchels of dimpled flesh that hung out on either side. This was at two in the afternoon, a few steps from the edge of the road. I had never seen that much of a woman's body before. Someone must have dared her, or maybe paid her to do it. I remember I stared for a couple of seconds because I knew she wanted me to look away, to feel ashamed.

When Guadeloupe had mentioned that Adeline had been there at the party, I'd been able to guess the nature of the unpardonable thing that Lucius had done. I didn't want to ask Adeline about that, but I thought maybe she could help by telling me how the injury had happened, and whether or not she believed Lucius was really dead. I dared to hope that my memory was wrong, that maybe he had only been unconscious and I had somehow revived him.

It was Sunday morning, Father Remy's turn for Mass, so I waited for him to trundle out into the church before I went outside to the car. From the church it's less than a mile to the edge of the reserve, along unpaved streets scored with petrified ruts that serve as memorials to the previous rain. The sporadic houses there were all built in the fifties but look much older: swagging rooflines, overgrown yards, ancient and illegal outhouses tilting dangerously. The town has never seen fit to provide water and sewer out there, hoping to keep its distance from the reserve. This policy ended up creating a miniature slum, nicknamed Little Chicago by the residents of Windfall who are fortunate enough not to live there.

The reserve begins on the far side of the river, but there is a cluster of bungalows on the town side too, and I had seen Adeline walking among them more than once. I drove slowly on the unnamed street, peering in the curtainless windows and inspecting the backyards. There were no fences here. Six boys rattled past on shaky bikes with hilariously small front wheels. It was going to be a hot day. Only the most resolute and decrepit of the shut-ins would stay inside this afternoon.

Adeline wasn't at any of her usual places, and it occurred to me that she might still be asleep, lolling in a lecherous dream in one of the nine houses on this side of the river. Sunday morning would not be a busy time for her. Most of her customers would still be sleeping themselves, or else attending church with their families. I drove back down the street, past one of the boys who was trying to put the chain back on his bike, and past a withered old man asleep in his truck, the scarlet visor of his ball cap jutting out the window like a flag.

I was trembling with hunger. I had eaten nothing but rice and consommé since my last encounter with Lucius and Guadeloupe. I drove to the highway and crossed the bridge to the Bi-Lo station on the reserve. The last time I had stopped at this place, years ago, there had been a café attached, but now the restaurant side of the building was boarded up. All they sold was chips and chocolate bars and greasy fried chicken that seemed to glow under an orange heat lamp. You could see the salt crystals on the skin, as if it wasn't meat at all but rather a mineral deposit, a chunk of ore. I salivated in spite of my better judgment, and bought a litre of Coke and a twelve-piece bucket of chicken. By the time I got back to the car, I had already devoured a drumstick.

I drove as slowly as possible, keeping my foot off the gas and letting the car idle down the dusty road that encircled the community. The vast swamp that serves as a water supply for Windfall was visible in the south, its viscid surface gleaming like something pure. Most of the houses on this side of the river were newer than the ones in Little Chicago, but they were still the same basic design. The Natives have tried to compensate for this enforced uniformity by painting the houses outlandish colours. Magenta is a popular one on our reserve, magenta with brown or green or yellow trim. Some of the older cars were done up in the same colours, applied with brushes or sometimes rollers.

I passed the band council office and the skating rink, and took the road nearest the river bank, reaching occasionally to grab another piece of chicken or to swill some Coke. This was what it felt like to cruise. I had never done it, even as a high school kid, because I had known from the age of fifteen that I was going to take holy orders. A middle-aged priest driving a K-car along a dusty and deserted road is hardly the quintessence of cruising, but it's the closest I've ever come. I leaned my left hand out on the rear-view mirror and steered with my right, a glazed and half-scarified piece of thigh meat hanging down from my fingers, dabbing against the steering column. I wondered how many other lonely men had cruised this street in search of Adeline.

There were a few more houses near the river bank, and then the street trailed off into a meadow. I stopped the car and got out, flinging a well-gnawed chicken bone into the grass, wiping my hands on my pants. There was no breeze. A stagnant, humid day. I reached in for the Coke and took a long pull, but I drank too fast and tears came to my eyes, refracting the sunlight into circles and hexagons of radiance. I sensed movement somewhere on the far side of the river, closed my eyes for a moment, looked again. Yes, it was Adeline, coming to me as if from a dream, stepping barefoot along the dirt path with a yellow towel draped over her neck. It was her usual place, but she wasn't here for customers this morning. I could tell by her clothes, the baggy sweatshirt and rumpled white boxer shorts that looked like they belonged to some man or other.

She didn't look across at me; she was too busy watching the path for rocks. I considered getting back in the car and driving around, but worried that I might lose sight of her, so I walked to the edge of the river bank instead. It was a steep twelve-foot drop to the river from my side of the bank, and there was no trail down, but I clung to a saskatoon bush and lowered myself to water level. I dislodged a piece of turf as I slid down, and it tumbled before me into the water, waving there in the current like a head of hair. Adeline heard the splash and squinted across at me.

"Hello," I said. "I've been looking for you."

"Yeah?" She didn't recognize me without my collar. She took the towel off her neck and shook it with one hand, as if cracking a whip. Her brown hair had been tinted the colour of dried ketchup, and it was pulled up into a voluminous pony tail.

"I need to ask some questions if you don't mind."

At this she suddenly looked into my face. Maybe she thought for a second that I was a cop, but then I saw the recognition coming to her. It seemed to melt her features like a guttering candle, elongating her overplucked eyebrows, pulling her waxy cheeks down toward the hollow semicircle of her mouth. I had expected a leer or a dirty joke or even another flash of her buttocks. This silence was unnerving. Finally she turned away and looked downstream, where several grey boulders were sticking up out of the water.

"I seen what you did to him," she said. "I went back there yesterday cause I didn't believe what people said."

I didn't answer for a while. My feet were sinking into the silt, and I could feel water coming in the front of my shoes.

"What *are* they saying?" I ventured.

She looked back at me, smirked. "The truth for once. Everything I heard was true. He was dead, now he's alive; he was a son of a bitch, now he's some kind of fucking saint. Or thinks he is. Calls himself Lazarus now. Lazarus Drake. I guess that makes you –"

"No!" I shouted. My voice echoed two, three, four times. I took a slow breath, and realized that Adeline had retreated several steps up the path. I had never imagined she could be frightened of anyone, least of all me.

"It doesn't make me anything," I said.

She scoffed, her hair bouncing like a squirrel's tail. "Don't tell me what it makes. I'm the one that seen him dead. No question about it, his tongue sticking out. It was all hard and purple like something in the butcher shop. His eye stuck open. We stayed for half an hour after it happened and he never took a breath, believe you me. I was listening for it."

I could only shake my head.

"Yesterday," she went on, "he was back to life. Praying and slobbering and howling with them goddamn dogs, but alive. I tried to talk some sense to him, but he just wailed about the Virgin Mary. 'Sing praises!' he'd say, and 'Alleluia!' like one of them preachers on TV. He said you were the one that done it, that brought him back, and I wasn't about to argue. Somebody sure as hell did."

She swung the towel back over her neck and turned away again, walking with her feet turned inward to avoid the rocks. I called out to her. The sound of her name was like a curse.

"Adeline!" I said again, and she stopped, but didn't turn around. I could imagine the look of exasperation on her face, the violent words forming. But I also sensed once more that she was afraid of me, like Lucius had been in the church. Maybe that was what made me do what I did.

"I have money…." I said.

We both stood without moving for a long moment, me with one hand on my wallet pocket, Adeline with her head cocked toward her right shoulder. I wasn't sure myself what I was proposing, but I didn't take it back. I left her to consider it. Finally she turned around and faced me squarely.

"What you did to him is disgusting," she said. "Un-natural." Her voice was low and furious. It seemed to push me back, physically, onto the overhanging turf of the river bank.

"You made him into a freak," she said. "A Jesus freak. And if you think you'll ever get those hands on me, living or dead, you better think again. I got protection you know. I got Vance to take care of me. And when I'm dead I want to stay that way. So stick your goddamn money up your ass for all I care, but leave me alone."

She ran away from me then, disregarding the rocks. The towel trailed out behind her left shoulder like a banner, and the blackened soles of her feet flashed rapidly at me. She was near the top of the hill already, making the turn toward the road. I leaped into the river to follow her, and I tried to run, but my feet sunk in the mucky bottom and I was held there, my body still moving forward into the current, my hands out punching through the surface and Adeline's hair eclipsed by the hill and the sharp slap of water in my face and the oil-drum sound of submersion. My eyes still open. Plumes of silt rising from my wrists like distant explosions. Lazarus. I had brought some-thing into the world and now it was going to cost me. One for one. It was pulling me down into the brackish water. I could no longer see my hands. I wrenched one foot out of the ooze and flailed it like a wounded octopus but still the other was stuck. The water was three feet deep, the mud bottomless. I could see the leathery skin of the surface, only inches above my head. The sun's algae-coloured nimbus bobbled in the sky, and fat balloons of air escaped from my nose. My eyes ached, so I closed them for a moment, reopened them again when I felt the black empty shape sliding up from wherever it had been hiding. It moved like plasma in my veins, a shape all darkness, come to extinguish the sun. I shrieked, releasing the last of my air in a flourish of coppery bubbles. I wondered what would happen to the sound. Would it be preserved in the bubbles until they reached the surface, bursting in a watery antiphon?

I waited. No use flailing now, too undignified. I asked the Lord to forgive me for the sins I had forgotten, and the ones I was unable to forget. Then I dared a quick gasp of water, to get it over with more quickly, maybe before the dark shape could do whatever it was going to do. One sip into my lungs, and that would be it. But when the water reached the back of my throat I couldn't make it go any further. I coughed, ragged empty coughs with nothing left in my lungs, and somehow the spastic motion pulled my leg free of the mud, and my face was suddenly in the air. I was floating on my back. For a second I didn't even dare to breathe, and then the inhalation began on its own, a ghastly sound like a great voracious machine with sand in the works. At the end of it, when my chest was inflated beyond any dream of its capacity, my head smacked against something hard. A rock. I reached back and dug my fingernails into the gelatinous film that coated it, then gingerly rolled

197

myself over until I was hugging the rock like a life preserver. About one square foot at the top of it was above the water, and I rested my chin there for a few seconds. The current was faster here, and it threatened to swing me back out into deeper water. I probed downward with my shoeless feet to find the bottom. It was only waist-deep, and solid enough as far as I could tell. I clambered up onto the rock and sat there cross-legged with my head sagging toward my lap. A monumental belch erupted from deep within me, reverberating in my entrails, echoing along the river bank. I was shocked at myself. But before I could take the full measure of my shame there was more coming out of me. I leaned out over the edge of the rock to vomit several great dollops of yellow matter, and then I watched it float slowly downstream, miraculously undiluted, like a vein of ochre. Drifting toward Lucius's place.

"Praise to you Lord Jesus Christ," I said, as if pronouncing a single word, and wiped my mouth on my sodden shirtfront. The white polyester was imprinted with swirls of mud and slime like a tie-dye gone bad. I shivered. Somehow I had managed to float most of the way across the river, even though I had only come about a dozen yards downstream. The rock I was sitting on was only six feet from the far shore, so I would be able to jump across to safety as soon as I regained control over my breathing.

Adeline was nowhere to be seen, nor was anyone else. I could hear voices coming from the houses, the birdlike sounds of children calling to each other, and half a mile futher down the river I could see the bridge, where a logging truck was crossing into town. Not one person had noticed me struggling there in the water, wrestling with the black shape of my destiny. It was hard to believe. I thought people were always watching me whether I wanted them to or not. But no, I could have sucked ten gallons of sludge into my lungs and died there, and floated downstream like a bloated cow trailing a procession of fronds and water cabbage behind me, and that would have been my funeral. Nobody would have known. And my body with its leafy entourage would have come to rest against the pilings of the old bridge, just down from Lucius's place, and it would have bobbed there in the current for weeks, retracing the same tired semicircle, until one hot afternoon it swelled up in the sun and exploded. And Lucius would have said a blasphemous prayer over the remains and burned the last of them in his rust-caked burning barrel until they vanished into a black cloud of soot. A shape all darkness. That was the only part of me that would have survived.

SATURDAY, JUNE 25
WINDFALL

I should have known: the abbey is not a separate world. I didn't have to wriggle through the eye of a needle to get there. But still I blame Lucius for the loss of it, my sanctuary, my refuge. If he hadn't forced his way back into my life again, I might be walking in those fragrant gardens right now, or praying at the Virgin's crèche, instead of huddling here in my room at the rectory, wondering when the Bishop or his agents will come knocking. I was just beginning to make progress, to understand what had happened between Lucius and me. My nightmares about the dark shape had not recurred for several days. Perhaps, in two or three more weeks, I could have built on those small victories and brought myself back to spiritual health. But Lucius prevented it. His three minutes on the evening news was enough to change everything.

I'm sure he doesn't care how his new notoriety has affected

me, even though he was praising my name with reckless abandon on the television screen, jumping up and down in the box of his truck while the ecstatic congregation looked on. I suppose he's congratulating himself on the free publicity. He'll make big money this time. The business of belief is the most lucrative one of all, and the easiest work. It isn't even illegal. I imagine he's already selling vials of moonshine and calling it holy water. Next will be keychains and cushions and plastic rosaries. Maybe he can even revive the Bird Zoo as a side show, something to amuse the faithful when they're tired of his fabricated miracles.

One thing I can be thankful for is that I was alone in the common room when Lucius came on TV. Everyone else was lingering at supper or preparing for Vigils. I had eaten early, as usual, to avoid the possibility of dining with someone who might have recognized me. I was sitting in a creaky recliner at the far end of the common room, reading an article in *Catholic Digest* about the shrine at Medjugorje. Someone before me had left the television on, and I was glad of the human sounds so I didn't switch it off. I wasn't really listening to the local news program that was playing, but still, the announcer's voice seeped into my consciousness. "You've heard of born-again Christians," he said, "but I doubt you've seen anything like this. Mr. Lazarus Drake, a one time farmer – now a preacher – claims to have risen from the dead. And his loose-knit congregation seems to believe him…."

At the mention of Lucius's name, I raised my eyes – slowly,

irrevocably – and regarded a scene that was so familiar I could almost believe it was a dream. It was exactly what I had witnessed when I'd caught him reading from Guadeloupe's Bible: the old truck parked on a hill in the hayfield, and Lucius standing there in the back, shaking his beard and proclaiming his tailgate prophecies. The only difference was that his dogs were no longer the only audience: there were *people* in the congregation – dozens of them. And as the camera panned through the crowd, I recognized that some of them were my parishioners. There was a close-up of Anna Lee Merasty, and one of Cyprien Fontaine. Old Mrs. Boulieu knelt in the front row, an arm's length from the endgate, her jowly face uplifted as if to receive a blessing. I could see in her eyes that she believed in him – that all of them did. The television reporter seemed to think the whole thing was a joke, but nobody in the audience was smiling. A parade of credulous faces moved across the screen. I had seen some of them countless times, peering up at me from the pews of Our Lady of Victory as I droned on in the pulpit about Christian duties and divine grace and the miracle of God's forgiveness. But I had never before seen that expression on their faces, that almost sexual look of open-mouthed, rapturous acceptance. I felt sick. These people had broadcast their sins to me in the fetid confessional for eleven years, and now here they were with the ache of sainthood on their faces, wanting to believe that I had performed a miracle.

They prayed right along with him, repeating his words like

a responsorial psalm. They sang praises in my name. And then someone produced a photograph of me and held it in front of the camera. It was one I had given to Guadeloupe a few months earlier: me wearing my collar and black shirt, standing near the cedars at the front of the church. My face was overexposed. I hovered there on the screen like a spectre, gazing out at myself with a half-expectant smile. For a moment I couldn't think at all. My whole body was clenched, and my breathing was almost unnoticeable. In the background I could hear the reporter talking about me: "Roman Catholic priest...not available for comment." And then it was gone. The reporter's face came back, his eyebrow raised in ironic comment as he summed up the imbecility he had witnessed. Then he too was replaced, this time by an advertisement: a loud-mouthed stereo salesman leaping around a showroom, pointing out his wares. Even in my state of shock, it entered my mind that this man was not very different from Lucius. He may as well have been selling snake oil or indulgences.

I was stunned for a while after this, unable to get up and extinguish the relentless television, which kept blathering on as if nothing had happened. Two retreatants walked past in the hallway, and I was terrified that they would come in and see me there, exposed, like a criminal in the stocks. This was enough to roust me out of my stupor. I listened to their footfalls until I heard two doors close, and then I leaped up and scuttled down the hall to my own room.

It was only when I got behind the locked door, with the blinds closed against the declining sun, that I was able to contemplate what had happened. I sat on the edge of the bed, imagining the thousands of people who had seen my photograph squinting out into their living rooms. Was Guadeloupe one of them? Father Remy? What about the Bishop? I knew that even if he hadn't seen it himself, someone would certainly inform him. And when he learned about it, he would want to push me further underground, into whichever ecclesiastical hideaway they reserve for the most errant and troublesome priests.

Perhaps I should have welcomed the thought of escaping forever from Lucius Drake and his ridiculous Novena, but my reaction was the opposite. I wanted to escape from the Bishop instead, because I knew he would only prevent me from facing up to the problems I was implicated in. Dozens of gullible people were going to lose their money and their dignity and possibly their immortal souls. I couldn't ignore it any longer, as the Bishop had encouraged me to do. I knew from the looks in those people's eyes that this problem was not simply going to fade away. It required action. The Novena had to be stopped, and I was the only one who could do it.

I arrived in Windfall on the bus late the next afternoon, huddled behind a newspaper and clutching my old wicker suitcase to my lap. I had left the abbey early in the morning when the monks were at *matins*, and I'd been lucky enough to hitch a ride to Saskatoon with an old couple who were going in for medical checkups. After a four-hour wait in an abandoned lot near the old power station, I had made my way to the bus depot and boarded the bus without any trouble. There were only a few other passengers, and none of them were my parishioners. As far as I could tell, no one had recognized me from television yet.

After the bus pulled into the depot I stayed in my seat for a few minutes, pretending to be asleep, in case any of my parishioners happened to be waiting for a parcel or a relative. When the driver came to wake me up, I had already peered out over the open cargo doors to verify that the sidewalk was clear. I stepped off the bus without so much as a sideways glance, and headed toward the church. I needed to borrow the pastoral K-car if I was going to get out to the Novena before the end of the weekend. Unfortunately, Father Remy had relieved me of the car keys before I'd left for the abbey, saying that he needed them in case he locked his own set in the vehicle. It was true that he often *did* lock them in, but still I wondered if this was part of the Bishop's plan to prevent me from having further contact with Lucius.

The streets of Windfall were deserted, except for stray dogs and children and the occasional snort of a logging truck moving down Railway Avenue on the outskirts of town. It was Saturday, and the weather was beautiful, so I imagined that most of the townspeople had gone up north to their cabins. Or else they were attending the Novena. That thought made me feel even more conspicuous. I had a horrible vision of being discovered by one of Lucius's believers and being forced to say prayers over someone's rheumatism. It made me want to shuffle furtively down the back alleys with my suitcase clutched to my chest, but I knew I would only draw more attention to myself that way. If I wanted people to avoid me, I had to walk purposefully and project the beaming confidence of a proselytizer or a vacuum cleaner salesman.

Instead of going straight to the rectory, I walked past the stampede grounds and out toward Little Chicago. I approached the church from the east, where I thought I could look in the rectory windows to get a better idea of what Remy was doing. From two blocks away I saw that the K-car was the only vehicle in the parking lot. I skirted a row of young maple trees and slipped into the doorway of our barn-shaped tool shed, which was the safest vantage point I could find. I crouched there beside a phalanx of garden utensils, assaulted by the smells of gasoline and fermented grass clippings that emanated from our riding mower. It was obvious that Remy hadn't cut the lawn since I'd left: the grounds were a thatched mess, like an unkempt hayfield, punctuated by hundreds of bobbing dandelions. As usual, Remy had taped a roll of tin foil up to the southernmost window of the library, to minimize the daytime heat. I could almost see in the kitchen window, but my view was obscured by reflections.

I checked my watch. Five-thirty. Usually by now he would have reached the nadir of his inebriation. It was often about this time that I would hear the bottle fall to the floor of his bedroom.

I waited a few more minutes, until the gasoline fumes had started to affect the clarity of my vision, and then I marched across the parking lot, still clutching my suitcase. I stopped at the screen door and peered momentarily into the dim catacombs of the rectory. When I saw no sign of Remy, I pulled on the handle – quickly, because I knew it was quieter that way. The door came back toward me with only the slightest groan. I stepped inside and stood there on the landing for a long minute, listening for Remy's shuffling footfalls, or the rusty complaint of his bedsprings, or even the doglike coughing sound that he made in the bathroom when he dredged up phlegm from the depths of his respiratory tract. I counted the toe-rubbers and galoshes and Hush Puppies on the rack beneath the heat register, and was relieved to see that all of them belonged to either Remy or me. The place had an unmistakable smell – something in addition to the obvious mixture of Remy's formaldehyde and dead animals and alcohol. It was a bachelor smell, a fug, intensely familiar but also disgusting, like the odour of one's own socks. I breathed through my nose in order to preserve the sanctity of my mouth.

Finally I made my way down the stairs and into the hallway that led past the library and the furnace room to the kitchen, where our key rack was located. I wondered why the hell we had put the rack down *there,* at the back of the bloody house. Why not in the porch like everyone else? I had never seen the illogic of this placement until now. I stopped at the edge of the library door, sniffed, and then looked around the door frame. The room was empty except for the mule deer and the squirrel and several of the songbirds that Remy had reassembled over the years, all of which were staring glassily back at me like demented sentinels.

I moved further down the hall toward the kitchen and stopped outside the entrance, leaning back against the wall, holding my suitcase out at an awkward angle to prevent it from banging on the gyproc. I listened for a while, and finally I edged my face around the corner and looked at the side of the cupboard, where the key rack hung. There was only one key on it, and even from that distance I could make out the yellow John Deere logo on the keychain. The riding mower. I wasn't going to get very far in that. I swore under my breath, cursing Remy and all his stupid machinations. He always kept his keys on that rack, unless they were locked in the car. And even *he* wouldn't have been able to lock both sets in there. I wondered if the absence of the keys was deliberate – if Remy had begun to take precautions against my reappearance. Had someone from the abbey already phoned to tell him that I had gone missing?

I was about to back out of there and make my escape when

I noticed something else in the kitchen, something distinctly out of place yet also immediately recognizable. A white woven cloth, carefully folded over the back of a chrome kitchen chair. I stepped quickly into the room, placed my hand on the textured fabric. There was a mosaic of raised shapes in the cotton: triangles and rectangles and stars. It was Guadeloupe's shawl, the one she had brought from Mexico, the one she had worn so many times in this room, when she came here after Mass for English lessons. I picked it up, held it to my cheek. It seemed like it was still warm.

She had to be there, somewhere in the building – though at first I didn't know what she might be doing there. Then I remembered what day it was, and I looked again at my watch. In an hour and a half, Saturday Evening Mass would begin.

Without a further thought about Remy, I stepped out of the kitchen and moved back down the hall to the furnace room, and from there I shuffled along the dank and musty passageway that led through the back of the chapel hall into the sacristy. My shoes were loud on the bare concrete, and my suitcase thumped against my thigh. I stepped up the three crumbling stairs into the sacristy, and as I entered the tiny anteroom I realized that Guadeloupe's shawl was still in my hand. I didn't know what to do with it. After a long hesitation, I stepped over to the vestry and laid the shawl out on top of the holy vestments. Then I turned toward the open doorway that led into the cavernous space of the church.

I looked out, first at the omnipresent crucifix along the back wall, and then toward the vacant altar, and finally down into the rows of empty pews arrayed like tombstones. The great wooden ribs of the church arched toward the apex of the ceiling. From the west, the sun flooded the stained-glass scenes of the Sermon on the Mount, the Passion, the *Pietà*. I forced myself to turn further to the right, so I could look past the edge of the pulpit toward Guadeloupe's pew, three rows in from the front. Sure enough, she was there, leaning forward with tiny elbows braced against the top of the next pew. Her hands were clasped in front of her head, which was bowed so deeply that she seemed to be looking back at her own torso. I could see only her shoulders, clad in a multicoloured gingham frock, and the thick black braid of hair that reached back between her shoulder blades. I watched the slow movement of her breathing, the rhythmic clenching and loosening of her delicate brown fingers. I said her name, tentatively, wondering if this was only an apparition, conjured by my own feverish necessity. But then she lifted her head, slowly – as if arising from an impossibly deep sleep – and there was no longer any reason to doubt. It was the same lovely face that I had known: the girlish, half-parted lips, the rounded cheekbones, the dark, unsettling eyes.

She didn't see me at first. I took a few steps forward and then stopped, uncertain what to do, what to say. I watched the recognition forming on her face: a sudden discomposure of her features, a tremor. I felt the reaction in my own body before I could begin to understand it. Something writhed in my stomach. What did she think of me? What had Remy been telling her? I remembered the last scene between the two of us, when she had driven me away like an unclean spirit.

She almost stood up, but it seemed like she couldn't move, as if she was caught between two opposing impulses. I thought I could see in her eyes a flicker of something other than fear, and I wanted to believe that it was love – that she too felt what I had so long felt for her. Perhaps that wasn't entirely a figment of my own desperate need at that moment to be loved, to be understood, to be forgiven. I know so little about such things. But I came to understand, in the long moment when we looked at each other, unmoving, like a pair of Father Remy's glass-eyed animals, that she herself no longer knew what she felt, or maybe even what she believed. She was infected with the same dark shape of doubt that inhabited me.

I wanted to explain what had happened, to somehow talk her back into the beautiful certainty that had once animated her features. I wanted to tell her everything that had happened to me. But I couldn't speak at all. Not there beside the altar with the crucified Christ looking down over my shoulder and the silent statue of the Madonna listening from her crèche beside the pulpit. The very emptiness of the church seemed to preclude the possibility of speech, as if there was not sufficient air in that vast space to serve as a medium for sound. I looked away from her, down the centre aisle toward the huge wooden doors at the main entrance. I could only think of one place where we would be safe to share our secrets.

Without another glance at her, I stepped down from the landing and began to move toward the back of the church. She and I had walked together up this same aisle on the first day I met her – the day that I had decided the direction of her pitiable life. There was still time yet for restitution.

I looked to the west, keeping my gaze away from her as I had always done before her confessions, to preserve the fiction of anonymity in the confessional. Mote-filled beams of coloured light came through the stained glass windows and projected their mottled and unrecognizable shapes onto the bare oak planks of the pews. Three votive candles were burning almost invisibly in the rack underneath the farthest window, their feeble illumination going completely to waste beside the brilliant effulgence of the glass. My back was to Guadeloupe now, but I could feel that she was watching me. I stepped over the huge wrought-iron heating grate at the end of the aisle, wondering if it would give way and plunge me into the sooty, lint-filled shaft that led back to the furnace. It held, of course, and I turned right, past the font of holy water with its sodden piece of sponge clinging to the nearest rim. When I reached my confessional, I stepped inside and pulled the door closed behind myself without looking back into the church.

She had heard me, I was sure, even if she hadn't turned

around to watch where I was going. I sat down in the musty chair, balanced my suitcase on my knees because there was no other place for it, and switched off the tiny night-light above my head. I have no idea how long I waited. Time is different in the darkness, when sleep is not a possibility and when you desperately want something to happen. All I could do was go over in my mind everything that I wanted to say to her. I repeated it all to myself, like an elaborate prayer, a litany, a whole rosary of self-revelation and imprecations and pleas for forgiveness. I would tell her everything that I had discovered about Lucius – how he was bilking innocent people of their money and their integrity. I would ask her to join me in my trip out to the Novena, where the two of us would unite in a refutation of the whole thing. I would give her a reason to believe in herself – and in me.

I felt safe there in the cloistered dark, for the first time in weeks. I remember thinking that even if Guadeloupe didn't come, I would still stay in there for hours on end, savouring my temporary respite from the troubles of the world.

But just as I thought this, I heard the familiar sound of the door on my right unlatching and swinging rustily open. The motion sucked some of the air out of my own cubicle, and then I sensed the shuffling of feet, the closing of the door, the creak of the *prie-dieu* as it accepted the weight of another penitent. I held my breath, preparing for the flood of syllables that she would produce when I opened the thin plywood window that separated us, and preparing for my own response – my fragile *mea culpa*, my plea for help, my desperate attempt to save her from the torment that I had experienced. There was no further sound in the confessional. I reached for the handle on the plywood and slid it fully open, as I had done thousands of times before, exposing the criss-crossed matrix of the wooden grate between us, the pattern of thin lathwork that always reminded me of a bank teller's window. And beyond it an unmoving, indistinct figure.

I had perhaps one second of certainty after I slid the window open, a precious moment in which I thought I knew what was about to happen. But then the whole situation slid away from me, and I was left with something entirely unforeseen. Maybe it was the sound, or the smell, or just the tension in the air. Whatever it was, it told me that something was wrong. And suddenly I understood, without squinting any further into the darkness, that this person kneeling a few inches away from me was not Guadeloupe. It was Remy.

I almost cried out – in shock, in despair. Even he seemed to cringe when I recognized him, as if he had been expecting some kind of reaction but was still surprised by the intensity of my anguish. I could only see his elbow and the ghostly outline of a dishevelled cassock that he must have pulled over his head while stumbling down the aisle, but it was enough. Far more than enough. The smell of his wine was unmistakable now, and I had to clench my throat against it to prevent myself from retching.

I was horrified by his presence, but far more disturbing to me was the absence of Guadeloupe. Where was she? What role did she have in this? I knew immediately that she must have told him, though I tried to force myself to deny it. She must have run to the rectory and awakened him from his wine-soaked dreams and shrieked at him until he stumbled over here to take charge of the situation. I could almost hear the hysterical legato of her Spanish imprecations as she pounded on his door to rouse him into action. It was this inevitable recognition that kept me from railing against Father Remy for all his deceits and malignancies. I knew I couldn't blame him for what Guadeloupe had decided about me. She had made up her own mind. This treachery belonged much more to her than to him.

Remy interrupted the vertiginous direction of my thoughts by beginning to speak. "Bless me Fodder, I have sinned," he said, just like he had done hundreds of times before in our sham confessions. I might have expected a tirade against clerical disobedience, or a lecture on the evils of the flesh, but not this. It was like nothing at all had happened. Except this time there was a strange, almost supplicatory intonation in his voice. I thought at first it was just the effects of the wine, but when he began reciting his Act of Contrition in the same earnest tone, I began to wonder. There was no irony in his voice, no malicious glee that he had caught me once again. He sounded like he meant it; like he *really was* heartily sorry.

At the end of his prayer, he went on with his confession at a slow, deliberate pace. He was drunk, but the words were sober. It was as if his drunkenness had allowed him to see the truth about himself, and to speak aloud the things that he had never been able to admit. I can't record here what he confessed, but I can say that for the first time in years, Father Remy made a sincere confession. He didn't gloss over his sins and imperfections as he had done before; he didn't hold back anything about himself. He even listed some of his trangressions against me.

I was almost as unsettled by this honesty as I had been by Guadeloupe's betrayal. I knew he must have had some kind of personal and spiritual reawakening during the time I had been away, and I found myself both awestruck and envious. But I couldn't answer back to him in kind; I couldn't ask him for reciprocal forgiveness. I was trapped in the role of the Father Confessor, and it was not possible to deviate from the official phrases that were required of me. The first time I spoke was to give him his penance, and then I pronounced the absolution with a dull sense of defeat. After that I hesitated, wanting to comment on his extraordinary performance, or to explain my presence there in the confessional, or even to tell him honestly about my plans for putting an end to the Novena. He didn't say anything either. The sound of air in his nostrils was like a tin whistle. I couldn't bring myself to start. I knew if I did, I wouldn't be able to stop until everything had been told, and I wasn't yet ready to tell everything. So instead of taking my own turn and telling him all the things I had been planning to tell Guadeloupe, I brought the confession to an end.

"Go and sin no more," I said.

This was when Remy looked at me for the first time. He leaned forward to catch me in the proper section of his bifocals. I thought I saw some mischief in his eyes even then, despite everything he had just admitted.

"And also with you," he said, and he made the sign of the cross with unconscious dexterity. Then he stood up, and the light in his cubicle came on, blinding both of us. I heard his feet shuffling unsteadily, and then the door clacked open and I saw the back of his wrinkled cassock as he ambled out into the church.

I shut the window on the empty compartment, enclosing myself once again in darkness, and I waited until I thought he would be starting his penance. Probably he heard me when I made my escape, but he didn't turn around from the pew where he was kneeling. No one else was in the church. I went out the back door and turned right, avoiding the parking lot in case any parishioners were coming early for Mass. I crept around the side of the rectory, and when I got in, I came straight up here to my room. There was no point looking for Guadeloupe. What I needed was to sit here on my bed, with the door locked, and write down everything that has happened. And decide what I will do tomorrow.

This is the third time Guadeloupe has denied me. The

final time. I know she has reasons, faulty though they are, but even so I can hardly believe she has done it. I was her only friend. She must have changed utterly. I guess everything changed for both of us the moment I placed my benighted hands on Lucius's face. Now, I'm overwhelmed with pity for her, despite my wounded pride, my aching sense of betrayal. If it hadn't been for Lucius's inadvertent resurrection, Guadeloupe would still believe in me. She might be facing manslaughter charges, or even murder, but she would still have her faith. She would know that what she did was justified before God.

Somehow, without intending to, I undid Guadeloupe's one act of vindication, of self-assertion, of vengeance. Or at least she thinks I did. In a way it doesn't matter what I feel about it anymore. I have become responsible – to Guadeloupe, and to every member of Lucius's deluded congregation – not because I did something, but because they believe I did.

There is only one way to save these unfortunate believers, and perhaps to save myself. I must go to the Novena, and stand there before Lucius, and finish what Guadeloupe began.

MONDAY, JUNE 27
THE BARRENLANDS

It was only yesterday that I left the rectory, swelled with right-eousness and the prospect of vindication. Now here I am, cry-ing in the wilderness – not as a prophet but an abandoned infant, exposed upon the heath, weeping my last pathetic notes before I fall forever asleep. No one can hear me. But before I commit myself to the wasteland's oblivion, I want to record how it happened, so that whoever finds me here will know the history of my struggle.

I didn't sleep at all the night before I left for Lucius's farm. I was embroiled in my imaginings of redemptive action, and I was also acutely aware of Father Remy's nocturnal movements in the bedroom beside mine. I could hear the springs of his bed every time he twitched, and I wondered if he was awake too, planning his phone call to the Bishop, or scheming about how to lock me in my room until the proper ecclesiastical authorities arrived. I was still disturbed by his confession as well. Sincerity was something I didn't expect from him, and as I went over the confession in my mind I began to wonder if it hadn't been ironic after all, or if it was simply part of his plot to delay me until the Bishop could be summoned. I felt trapped in my own room. Now that I had resolved to undertake a final confrontation with Lucius, I became terrified that Remy would do something to prevent it. I lay there on my bed, fully clothed, ready to charge out the door and down the stairs at the first sign of treachery.

The pre-dawn light became visible just after three in the morning, and I decided to leave then because I could no longer contain my paranoia. I took my suitcase and my notebook, perhaps sensing that I might not return. I made another cursory search for the car keys in the kitchen, but I knew Remy would be keeping a close watch on them so I didn't waste much time looking. I had thought of an alternate form of transportation in any case. The river flowed past Lucius's place, and I remembered having seen an old canoe along the bank in Little Chicago.

There was no need to worry about being seen by anyone at that time of the morning. I walked up the road to Little Chicago without even awakening a dog. All was quiet when I got to the river, and the canoe was still where I had remembered seeing it, overturned beside a cluster of dead willows near the bank. It was dark green fibreglass, bleached a lighter colour on one side from years of exposure to the sun. I pried it out of the underbrush and flipped it over, revealing a maze of anemic grasses underneath. There were no paddles, so I broke off a long, stout willow branch and stripped away its twigs to create a makeshift punting pole.

I dragged the canoe down to the water and pushed off like a gondolier, trying to look nonchalant, to seem like I had every right to do this. The boat might have belonged to any of the residents of Little Chicago – even Adeline or her protector Vance. All the more reason for caution. As I moved out into the oily current, I poled a few more times, and then I sat down on the mildewed slats of the seat. There was still a slight haze of fog clinging to the river, but I could see well enough to avoid the exposed rocks and sandbars and deadheads. The water was fairly low, which meant there would be more obstacles to dodge, but it also meant I wouldn't have to worry about rapids.

I moved almost silently on the fish-smelling water, leaning occasionally on the pole to correct my course. Sometimes I couldn't touch the bottom, and I was entirely at the mercy of the current. At such times I lifted the pole into the boat and resigned myself to the whims of the water, floating sideways or even backwards until I saw that I was nearing a shallower spot. If anyone had seen me emerging from the fog, drifting broadside down the river with my head lifted stoically and my pole resting across the gunwales, they would have wondered what kind of creature I was. A castaway. A middle-aged Moses looking for bulrushes. A deluded Charon, inconceivably off course, drifting down to meet his own obliteration. Certainly, no one would have asked me for a ride. But the only witnesses to my passing were the flocks of pigeons that burst out terrifyingly from beneath every bridge I passed, dropping salvos of guano into the water. Sometimes it floated along beside me for several minutes.

It was not long before I drifted beyond the last of the neon-coloured reserve houses and into open rangeland. I had heard there were hill-billies who lived in caves along the river bank up here, scions of a renegade band of squatters who had migrated from Kentucky in the fifties. Lucius was probably one of them – but a more civilized one, since he actually owned some land and had a house with electricity. And he hadn't married his sister. It was strange to think that in some quarters, Lucius might actually be a shining example of worldly success. Luckily for me, I didn't see any caves in the muddy bank, though I did pass by several shoddy tar-paper dwellings that made Lucius's hovel look like a lord's manor.

I hadn't accounted for the interminable switchbacks in the river's course, so it took much longer to reach Lucius's place than I had imagined. After an hour I lost all perspective on my location. The fog eventually lifted, and it was replaced by clouds of insects that seemed hell-bent on drowning themselves in my eyes. Finally the little monsters were driven away by the heat of the sun, but after half an hour of solar radiation blasting on my forehead, I wished I could go wherever the insects had gone. In an effort to ward off heatstroke, I took an undershirt out of my suitcase and wrapped it around my head like a turban. Even so, by eleven o'clock my thirst and delirium were strong enough that I lost all fear of waterborne diseases. I took the turban off, dipped it in the murky river, and sucked on the cloth. It tasted like the dregs of a neglected aquarium.

I floated for another hour before I heard the first sign of the Novena: a sharp metallic voice echoing across the water. Someone with a megaphone, possibly Lucius himself. Then it stopped, and I heard the vague, hulking, almost inhuman uproar of the crowd's response. I began poling more urgently whenever I could touch bottom. Finally I rounded a horseshoe corner, and the pilings of the old bridge came into view downstream. Up on the bank, between Lucius's buildings and birdcages, was a shantytown of fifth-wheel trailers, vans, tents, and lean-tos. It seemed like these dwellings had been carefully chosen to complement Lucius's already extensive collection of wrecks. Makeshift clotheslines were slung in the trees, and Hibachis and coolers and cook stoves were scattered around the encampment. At first I could see no people, but then I drifted past a woman who was squatting in the bushes down by the water. I averted my eyes before either of us could recognize the other.

I moved past the whole circus-like assembly, unnoticed

except by the flustered woman in the underbrush. Though I couldn't see the congregation, I imagined that they were assembled in Lucius's usual place: the hayfield behind the house. The megaphone was silent now, and I could only hear a generalized tumult of voices which came from no particular direction. I poled myself to shore just in front of the cluster of accumulated brush at the bridge pilings, where the dead cow was conspicuous by her absence. I wondered if she had sunk beneath the debris or if she had decomposed enough to wash through the tangle of branches. There was no rope to tie the canoe down, so I pulled it up out of the water and wedged it between two pieces of dessicated driftwood. Then I climbed halfway up the bank and peered above the overhanging turf. I waited a full minute to be certain that my way was clear. Finally, I pulled myself up onto the grass and walked toward the house, stepping uncertainly between the parked vehicles and empty bird cages, wondering what I would say if I bumped into someone who recognized me. The congregation began its chanting again, saying "Pray for us" in a zombified tone. The prayer leader reacted with a fury of high-pitched words through the megaphone, stinging the crowd into each response. I passed the unfinished barn and found the foot-path, which had now been widened into a highway by the passage of hundreds of believers. The forest along the path reeked of urine and the dizzying pong of furtive defecation. Lucius might claim to be able to feed the multitudes, but he certainly hadn't performed any commensurate septic miracles.

Someone was coming, so I stepped off the path and stumbled into the bush, pretending to be one of the legions of urinators who had gone before me. It was a woman and child, and neither of them seemed to recognize me, so I continued through the bush, breathing as infrequently as possible. I decided to stay in there, no matter how much the ammonia hurt my eyes, until I had conducted a reconnaissance of the whole gathering. I moved toward the edge of the field and looked down at the assembly: hundreds of people, shoulder to shoulder, forming a great teeming circle around Lucius's truck. They were kneeling in the dirt with their hands clasped and their eyes closed. The dogs loped around the perimeter of the crowd, as if to keep the herd in prayer formation.

In the back of the truck with Lucius were two other men, one of them wearing a suit, the other a buckskin jacket and jeans. Lucius was still wearing the same plaid shirt he had died in. The man in the suit was leading the prayers, calling out through his bullhorn like an auctioneer, "HolyMary-MotherofGod," and the crowd responding "Pray for us!" This man was wearing oxblood cowboy boots and he spoke with a slight accent, like a country singer. He was the only one of the whole multitude with his eyes open, and he surveyed the crowd like a fifth grade teacher looking for troublemakers. Lucius had his hands clasped over his paunch, and he was muttering to himself as if preparing to speak in tongues. The man in the buckskin said nothing at all, but his face held an expression of puzzlement, as if he had just awakened to find himself transported into the middle of this throng. His blonde hair was unkempt, and he shuffled from side to side in the truck box, jostling against Lucius and the other one. He peeked out his right eye every few seconds to see if the people were still looking at him. Beside him, Lucius suddenly thrust his hands up into the air and shook his bristly beard like a blind prophet.

I backed into the bush again and walked along the edge of the field about a dozen steps. One of my parishioners, Dennis Chorney, was standing near the back of the congregation, his pudgy face wracked with ecstasy as he cried out "Pray for us" in a continuing crescendo. The man in the suit changed his refrain to "JesusChristLordofPeace," and the people responded more loudly than ever. Charismatics, I thought. Even though I had seen it on TV, I was more shaken by this display than I had expected. These people *believed* that Lucius had come back from the dead. And that I was responsible.

The man suddenly stopped speaking, but the crowd said "Pray for us" two more times before he brought their momentum under control. Then everyone was quiet, and the people opened their eyes to look at the unlikely triumvirate standing in the lopsided truck box. The man put the megaphone down at his feet, and then addressed the crowd in a more reserved and clerical manner.

"And now my friends in Christ," the man said, "it is time

228

to hear a testimonial from one of our brothers, a fellow sinner who has turned toward the Lord because of Lazarus. He was a witness to the death of Lazarus, and he is here to recount for us the first part of the miracle. Brother Percy, will you tell us what happened?"

The man in the buckskin stepped toward the tailgate and nodded toward the other one. "Yes I will, Mr. Bernier. I'm not a talker by nature, but I want to tell these people what I seen, so they can believe the way I do, so they can know the truth about Lazarus Drake and the miracle that happened to him."

Percy stopped for a while and looked out into the crowd as he tried to decide where to start. Some of the audience called out encouragement to him, and finally he began again.

"Now I'm not one to judge another man," he said, "so I won't tell you about the things I seen ol' Lucius Drake get into. Trouble I mean. No end of it. And I was no better. We egged each other on, I guess. But one night it all come to an end. There's no need to describe the sins we committed and the ones we were planning that night, but I'll just say that we were at our worst.

"And then his wife – God bless her – she come at him from behind." He shifted uneasily as he spoke, unbalancing the springs in the truck box. "And I was sitting on the other side of the table, I seen the whole thing. But didn't have time to do nothing. She come out of nowhere swinging this gun by the barrel, and it caught him just above the eye, and he fell like a tree. He fell over in his chair and I remember his feet were sticking straight up in the air, like if you nailed a boot to a fencepost."

He paused to produce a goofy grin, but the people in the crowd were not in a mood for humour. They were revisiting a miracle, witnessing a passion play, and every moment was utterly serious.

"And we went to him and stood over him, but his eyelids were fluttering, like the way an animal does when it dies. A bird or what have you. I seen it a thousand times. I knew he wasn't just knocked out, I knew it right away, and I said 'I think he might be dead.' And his wife says, 'yes,' like she knew it was going to happen. And we picked him up and laid him on the table, and took turns listening at his mouth for breath, but there wasn't any. He was dead. We stayed for half an hour, and in all that time he never took a breath or had a heartbeat. Then we got scared, I'm ashamed to say it. We thought the police might be coming, and we took off for home."

The man in the suit interrupted him. "He's ashamed, do you hear that my brothers and sisters? But he was a witness to a miracle, the first part of the great miracle of resurrection. Because if Lazarus had not died, he could not have risen again!"

They cheered this with abandon, shouting and clapping and exulting until the whole place became an embodiment of noise, a whirling tornado of sound. They called for Lazarus to speak, and the man in the suit couldn't quiet them down for a long time. Finally he shouted "Lazarus will pray!" and the crowd exploded into alleluias again. They only went silent when Percy stepped back away from the tailgate and Lucius came forward, nodding his head and smiling benevolently at his followers. He looked slowly from side to side as if he was counting them, or perhaps calculating the amount of money he could squeeze out of them. His lips trembled as he warmed up to speak.

"This is the forty-third day of my Novena, my prayer of thanks for the life that was given to me, not once but twice. This is my new life. In the old one I was an instrument of the devil, but now my life is the Lord's."

Some of the congregation burst out with spontaneous alleluias, and Lucius waited for the noise to abate. When the crowd was silent again, he stood absolutely still for at least ten seconds, his head cocked to the side as if listening for the inspiration of God to enter his left ear. Then suddenly and dramatically he began, leaning forward into the crowd as if to tell them a secret.

"It was like this: I was a wicked man. Many of you knew me from before, and all of you heard about me. So I don't need to convince you. When it came to ungodliness, I done everything there was to do, and I invented a few more things that nobody'd thought of before. I stole. I lied. I hurt people. I hurt the Lord Jesus Christ himself. I *maimed* him. Many times.

Because every one of my sins was like another nail in his flesh, another thorn in his crown, another blade in his side. Every time I hurt someone, the Lord felt that pain a thousand times deeper than any of us could know.

"The devil, he was on me like a shadow, following along in the tracks of my sins, laughing like a coyote. He knew I was fine material. You'd think the Lord would have just let me go, written off my soul, like the bankers sometimes do with bad debts. I was too far gone in sin. But the Lord doesn't think that way – that's the beauty of it. *Nobody is too far gone.* If I wasn't, then none of you are neither.

"He sent two messengers to show me that I needed to change my ways. One was my wife and the other was a priest, a man I hardly knew. My wife, she gave me a taste of death. And I thank her for it, from the bottom of my soul. I was in the depths of my wickedness, I had done every thing there was to do, and I was trying my damndest to drag her into it all. To make her as wicked as I was. But she wouldn't have none of it.

"That night, like Percy said, she came to me like an avenging angel, and she struck me down. And I died right there at the table, with evil thoughts in my mind and a bottle of whiskey in my hand and an unclean woman sitting beside me.

"You know how I knew I was dead? Because there was nothing. Nothing! No dreams. No tunnel of light like some people say, no floating away from my body, no chorus of angels. I didn't see the face of God because I didn't deserve to.

There was only a wisp of me left, enough to understand one thing: *this nothing is the entryway to hell.* I was sliding, like as if some motherlode magnet of the soul was pulling at me, dragging me further into that nothing, and soon I would vanish completely, and reappear in the world on the underside of this world. Which the Bible calls hell.

"But that was not to be. Even though I deserved it. Because the Lord in his all-powerful and ever-living mercy had different plans for me. He had not given up, not even on a miserable, wicked, unrepentant sinner like me. Oh no. He had not given up.

"I was saved by a great holy man who became the instrument of the Lord – a man who placed his hands upon me and called my soul back to this earth. There is no explaining it. Like every other miracle, all we can do is believe. Father Silvan touched my forehead with his hands and summoned all the power of the Father and the Son and the Holy Spirit to come into me and drag me back from the edge of nothingness. And when I awoke and saw the two of them there, my wife and Father Silvan, I knew that they had worked together, through the power of the Lord, to give me a second chance. I changed my ways right then and there. I became a new man entirely. That's when I devoted myself to this Novena.

"And when the Lord calls me home again, I'll be ready. No more of that nothing for me. No more sliding and sliding toward that pit of hell. Because I have prepared me a way for the Lord Jesus Christ to enter my heart. And he will lead me out of that valley of darkness and take me to the place where lions and lambs lie down together. The place of plenty. The place we all want to go to when our time comes."

He paused for a moment. I had walked up to the edge of the crowd to listen, since I saw that they were all mesmerized by him and there was no chance they would recognize me. I had stood there at the perimeter of the congregation for most of the speech, feeling the intensity of the crowd, the amazing credulity with which they hung on his every word. I had been drawn into it myself, not by the content of what he'd said but by the oracular cadences, the stunning power of his voice. He had become far more sophisticated in his methods of chicanery. I was in awe of that, and in awe of the control he had over the crowd. If only my parishioners had listened to my sermons with a fraction of the attention that they gave to the inflated words of this charlatan.

There were several points in his speech where I had wanted to interrupt him, to yell out to the people that he was lying, that all he really wanted was their money. I had been planning to sway them to my side before I carried out my ultimate purpose. But I was unable to raise my voice against the conviction of his sermon and against the solid bulwark of belief that the congregation had erected. I saw that I might have to act on my own, before a throng of hostile witnesses.

It was then, as he swept his glance over the crowd, perhaps

formulating a stirring conclusion to wring every shekel from the astonished believers, that he recognized me. The surprise seemed to paralyse him for a second, and then he stepped forward in the truck box, to the edge of the tailgate, squinting and holding his breath. The truck wallowed on its flimsy springs when he moved, and the other two men were thrown off balance. They steadied themselves gingerly before looking in the direction of Lucius's gaze.

The crowd was silent, and some of them pivoted their heads back toward me. Gasps came out of them like the sound of air brakes.

"I said he would come," Lucius announced, almost tentatively, as if he still wasn't sure that it was me. There were exclamations of rapture from the crowd, and a tumultuous rumble of questions for me and for the men in the truck box. The people were wondering where this appearance fit into the program.

Lucius was still staring at me with an expression I have only seen on paintings of the apostles. It was frightening, the sincerity in that face. I had always considered him a consummate deceiver, but now I had to wonder if he could fake such piety. For a moment I almost thought that he truly believed in me. I had been hoping that my sudden appearance might cause him to falter, and that this would allow me to discredit him. But I was the one who faltered when I saw the earnestness in his face – especially when I saw how it contrasted with the cynical alarm in the face of Mr. Bernier, the man in the suit. I could see that this turn of events didn't fit into any of *his* plans, and he was wondering what he could do to keep the situation under control.

Before the suit man could think of anything, though, Lucius dived headfirst into the crowd like a rock musician at a stadium show. The believers nearest the endgate caught him, and the crowd rose up in one stupendous motion, with a sound like the wings of a thousand birds. They cried out something I couldn't comprehend, the language of true believers. Then they surged toward me, and though I stepped back in terror I was swept up with them before I could do anything to escape. Suddenly I was above them, hovering on their fingertips, held aloft by the very force of their belief. The sound was deafening. I moved against my will toward the shaggy form of Lucius Drake, who was rocketing at me with uncanny precision. I could have believed that the end of the world had arrived, and that Lucius and I were ascending together and the rest of them were waiting below for a less happy reward.

Then Lucius was upon me, and he closed me in his foul and bearish arms, and his beard pressed against my face, and I felt his tears on my own cheek. The crowd held us there for a long time, and Lucius continued to weep, and I smelled the rank perfume of his lucky clothes. He was speaking to me, confessing his secrets, but I couldn't hear for the noise of the crowd. Finally I began to regain myself, and I twisted away from him. I caught a glimpse of the man in the suit, still standing there in the distant truck box, waving his arms and raging against the hysteria that had taken the crowd away from him. I knew then that the lot had fallen to me.

"I've come to baptize you," I yelled to Lucius, and some of the people below us must have heard me, because they began to repeat that word, baptize, until it became a refrain.

"To the river!" I screamed, and Lucius responded, "The river!" and the crowd began to move once again, holding us above their heads like bags of grain. We were on the path now, Lucius pulling ahead and myself following the slick soles of his workboots, and the people chanting something I couldn't understand. We tumbled headlong toward our destinies at the hands of a maniac crowd.

When we arrived at the river bank, the multitude deposited both of us on the ground, side by side. They spread themselves out along the bank and stepped back from us. The hysteria diminished as suddenly as it had erupted, and I stood there looking at Lucius, trying to catch my breath. He gazed back at me, his shoulders slumped, his palms turned outward as if to exhibit stigmata. But his saintly masquerade only disgusted me. After everything he had done to these people, and to Guadeloupe, and to me, he still had the gall to stand there without a hint of shame on his face. I hated him for that, and for coming back to life, and for infecting me with the dark shape of despair.

He was a large man, a very powerful one. And yet I was not afraid of him, or of the mesmerized crowd that watched us with desperate expectation. I was an instrument of justice. All decisions were behind me; there was only one thing to do.

"I've come to save your followers," I said.

The crowd cheered at this, and new tears bloomed in Lucius's beard. He had lost his precious Bible somewhere in the melee, but his memory proved sufficient for a paraphrase of scripture:

"The Lord giveth and He taketh away," he said. "Though I walk in the valley of the shadow of darkness, I shall fear no evil."

I could think of no more appropriate proverb for the occasion, so I placed my hand on Lucius's shoulder and led him down the slope of the bank. We paused at the edge of the water, and I looked back at the spectators assembled there, every last one of them holding their breath. Then I waded out into the river, three steps. It was a steep bank; I was already up to my waist and I continued to sink in the mud. I turned back toward Lucius and opened my arms to him, and he stepped forward without removing his boots or his heavy plaid shirt. I could feel the sludge of the river bottom enclosing me. Lucius waded slowly, with a great sense of drama, as if he believed he might be able to walk on water. But he sank down just like me, and when he reached me he turned around and leaned backwards into my outstretched arms, as if to practise the limbo.

I was shivering. The current pulled against my legs and my lower back, and the weight of Lucius's torso pushed me deeper into the mud. His head hung past my left arm, his hair floating wildly in the water, his eyes still open, staring up at me with a terrifying sense of trust.

"Go on," he whispered, and I did. I lowered him into the murky river and it closed over his face. His eyes were still open, staring not at me but at something above me in the sky. I removed my hands from under his back and pushed down against his chest, fighting against his buoyancy. He lay there serenely, not fighting back, not thrashing up to the surface. His features were blurred by the mucky water, and his face was distorted by the swirls in the surface so that it looked like something from a dream. He was strong enough that he could have stopped me, I knew that. But he didn't try. I pushed harder, wanting to make him disappear in the depths, but still I could see him, his hair waving like a fright mask, his eyes wide. I pictured him holding Guadeloupe down like this in their bed, forcing her to acquiesce. He had to pay for his transgressions. He could no longer escape her vengeance.

I counted as slowly as I could, the sound of my heart in my temples, the calls of people from the river bank coming to me from a great distance. A flurry of bubbles swarmed out of his mouth and erupted soundlessly at the surface. It smelled of his breath. Still I held him down, I held him down with all the force of my will and all the strength of my conviction. Because

I knew I had to, because it was the price of my faith. It was the only way to set things back to the way they should have been. I remembered Abraham at the altar, the plunging knife. The hand of the angel.

But I knew, even as I thought this, that I was no Abraham. God had not spoken to me. I looked down into Lucius's swollen and distorted face, and even then I saw the sincerity in it, the raw belief that I had craved so much. I thought of his willingness to trust in me. My own sense of certainty wilted in comparison. I couldn't be sure that what I was doing was right. I looked down at my hands, at the terrible ministry they were performing, and the word murder came into my mind and circled there like the dark shape of my doubts. I faltered. I let go of him, and he floated up to the surface and bobbed there like an empty bottle. And inhaled.

I was stunned at my failure. I stood there chest-deep in the swampy liquid, unsure if I should duck down into the river and finish my piteous life, or allow the crowd to tear me apart. Lucius was still floating, and some of the believers had dived in to pilot him to shore. The multitudes gathered around him, leaning over the bank with their hands on each other's backs like a human pyramid. All of them were watching him. They didn't seem to notice me at all.

My canoe was still on the bank where I had left it, thirty yards downstream. I leaned back in the water and released myself into the current, tugging my feet up out of the mucky bottom, drifting along almost dreamily, watching the spectacle on the bank as if I had played no part in it. The congregation had forgotten my existence. They had pulled Lucius up into a standing position, and two of the men were hammering on his back. I heard him coughing convulsively. They asked him questions and he shook his head feebly.

My drifting stopped when I came to rest against the brush-pile in front of the old bridge. I was suddenly terrified of the missing cow, and I frantically pulled myself to shore, clinging to twigs and branches and broken fenceposts. I crawled up out of the slime, my shoes missing, my pants slipping down my legs, and I dragged the boat along the bank to the far side of the pilings. I launched it quickly, spinning sideways into the current. By this time some of the crowd had noticed me, and they yelled at me to come back. A few of them even followed me along the bank for about a hundred yards, but they stopped when the man in the suit called them off. He told them to leave me alone because I was unworthy.

It was the right word, but wrongly applied. I am unworthy of God. I am an emptiness now. I have failed Him for the last time.

I floated for most of the night, shivering through swamps and over beaver dams and past uncaring herds of cattle. When I ran aground for the hundredth time I couldn't bear to stay on the water any longer. I stepped ashore, and took my battered suitcase and my notebook along. Then I pushed the boat off without me.

I've been living in this abandoned granary for almost a day now. I listen to the mice hurrying back and forth to their dens, and I watch through holes in the walls for the hawks that hang in the breeze above the hayfield.

Sometimes I'm roused from my tormented slumbers by the unearthly wail of the coyotes. They are scavengers. Perhaps they are calling me.

I thought the vigilante believers would have found me by now, but maybe they have listened to the man in the suit. Maybe they have washed their hands of me, since in the end I did no harm to their leader. All I did was give him a new reason to claim victory over death. It's as if I had saved him again.

THURSDAY, JULY 7
HOME

I had thought I would make no more entries. By now I should be nothing but an unearthly stench seeping through the walls of a long-abandoned building, or an excuse for a hypocrite funeral at Our Lady of Victory, with half a day of bells and truckloads of flowers and Father Remy, drunk with glee, homilizing me to hell. Sorry to have disappointed him. It was not by my own design. It happened, as usual, through outside intercessions.

I stayed in my granary for three days, sleeping in a pile of hay that I'd pulled from a dishevelled bale stack. I had learned that I was nothing but an empty shape, a form without content, and I waited for the zealot mob to find me and put an end to my suffering. I sat in my corner day and night, listening to the wind, watching the shadows change as the light came through the holes in the walls. Mostly I slept, without dreaming. Since that time I have not been able to dream.

Whenever I awoke, I heard the mice and rats moving about the place as if I wasn't there at all. My back became knotted with cramps from sleeping on the hard plank floor, and I shivered continually because my clothes were still damp from my swim in the river. But I made no effort to alleviate these discomforts. Nor did I bother looking for food, though at times my stomach seemed to be devouring me from within, and I chewed on my shirtsleeve for solace. Thirst was the only affliction that drove me from my self-appointed sepulchre: once each day I stumbled down to the river and drank handfuls of sludgy water. It gurgled in my intestines for hours afterward, like something alive.

I didn't dream, but as I waited there in the dark for the great unknown to close in upon me, I was plagued with memory. Again and again I remembered Guadeloupe looking up at me from her pew, and the fear that had transformed her face as she recognized me. I felt my grandmother's deathbed hands on my arm. I saw the murder of crows swarming in a column above me like a plume of smoke. The outline of Father Remy's face in the confessional, and the smell of his Christ-soaked breath. I saw Lucius Drake coming back to life and lurching upright on the edge of his kitchen table. I felt the charge of negative energy that had travelled through my arms into him. And most of all I witnessed the empty humanoid form that had waded down and down into my consciousness just before that energy had been released. As I lapsed further into delirium, this horrifying image of the shape all darkness was the one that recurred most often. Whenever I felt it coming, I was wracked with convulsive movements in my arms and legs – a desperate bodily attempt to escape. I came to believe that the dark shape was myself, that I had been haunted all along by the spectre of my own emptiness. I huddled there in the timeless dark, dreading each coming visitation.

It was late afternoon on the third day when Lazarus found me there, shivering beneath the mound of hay. I didn't hear him coming. All I remember is the terrible brightness of the sun when he opened the door. The pain of it brought tears to my eyes. His bearded face hovered above me, and he spoke some quiet words that I was unable to interpret. I couldn't tell if he was real or if this was a vision, a nightmare of abduction orchestrated by the dark shape within me. I felt utterly disconnected from my body when he slid it out from under the hay and arranged my arms on my chest. He kept speaking the whole time in a gentle reassuring tone, like you might use when approaching a wounded animal. He lifted me awkwardly, and staggered out of the granary with my body cradled in his arms. I remember the warmth of him against my side, and the sound of his laborious breathing. The truck was not far away, but the ground was uneven and clogged with vegetation, so he had to put me down twice. I was unable to help him or to struggle against him. I wasn't sufficiently aware of myself to have an opinion about whether I wanted to go or not. Finally he lifted me up into the passenger seat and propped me there, and then took an oily canvas tarpaulin out from behind the seat and arranged it over me like a blanket. He handed me a Mason jar half full of sun-heated water, and I drank greedily, breathing through my nose between swallows. By the time I had drained the last of the pickle-smelling liquid, he had gone back to the granary and returned with my suitcase and my notebook.

The next thing I remember is waking up in his house with the hot breath of dogs in my face. They were eyeing me with that peculiar brand of sympathy that only dogs can muster: watery eyes, wrinkled brows, occasional whines of commiseration. Lazarus was not in the room, but I recognized the place immediately. I could see part of the kitchen through the open door: two chrome chairs and the edge of the arborite table where he had been laid out. Beside me was a half-empty closet with some of Guadeloupe's cotton dresses dangling from the metal hangers. I was lying in their bed.

My primary sensation was hunger. I would have eaten the dogs if I could have caught them. But I could hardly move, so I huddled there in the foul-smelling blankets, conserving my miniscule resources of energy. I thought about Lazarus. It seemed that he had saved me, at least for the moment, though I didn't know whether to bless him or curse him for it. Why had he gone to such trouble, after what I had tried to do?

Maybe he wanted to punish me by prolonging my death, keeping me barely alive for days on end. Perhaps he would keep me a prisoner until the Novena was over, so I wouldn't spoil the racket.

Sometime later I heard the dogs scrambling toward the other room, and then the screen door slammed. I turned over to see Lazarus standing in the kitchen, peering in at me, his face twisted into the same look of puzzled compassion I had seen on the dogs. Neither of us spoke. Then he disappeared behind the edge of the door and I heard him lumbering about in the kitchen for several minutes, and I recognized the half-forgotten smell of cooking. Eventually he reappeared at the threshold of the bedroom, holding a plate of boiled cabbage and fried balogna.

All I could muster was a single syllable. "Why?"

He stood there for a long time without answering. Wisps of steam came off the translucent clumps of cabbage.

"Because you're in need," he said. "It's like the Lord says about the Samaritan and such. Except you're not my enemy. I wouldn't even be here without you."

"Not true," I said. But he looked so sure of himself that I couldn't argue any further.

"It's what the Lord would want," he added.

I had no energy left to contradict him, so I motioned for him to bring me the food. He sat down on the bedside and spooned the bland morsels into my mouth. I barely stopped to chew. When I was finished he went out to the kitchen and returned with a bowl of soup. There was a thick scum of fat on top, and a splintered beef or pork bone sticking out, and clots of marrow skulking on the bottom. I ate it without question or complaint, and when I was finished, my body overwhelmed my will and I slid back into the limbo of sleep once again.

It was like that for several days. I was too weak to question him, too delirious to fully comprehend my situation. At first I was terrified that the crowds from the Novena would learn I was there and would come after me seeking retribution, but when Lazarus understood the source of my fear he explained to me that the Novena had been postponed, and that it would remain so until I decided otherwise. I didn't want to speculate about his reasons for doing this, but I took him at his word, and this enabled me to relax a little. Most of the time I slept, wrestling with my memories as I had done before in the granary. The dark shape still visited me here, but it seemed almost reluctant, as if the presence of another person could keep it at bay.

Lazarus slept in the kitchen, on a mouse-ridden mattress that he had dragged in from one of the outbuildings. He fed me and brought me tea, and emptied the old tin chamberpot that he had left, tactfully, beside the bedstead. In short, he tended to me with a devotion I had never thought possible. I suppose he had learned his nursing skills from all his years as a dog healer. For all I knew, the food he gave me was the same thing he was feeding his dogs, but I didn't mind. I devoured it with enthusiasm. After the first day I was able to feed myself, so he just brought me the plates and sat there on the side of the bed watching me eat. It seemed to make him happy. We rarely spoke, but I could tell that he saw his nursing duties not as an obligation but as an opportunity, a chance to repay his imagined debt to me, and also perhaps to prove something about his own sincerity.

He was often gone for one or two hours at a time, doing chores, or talking to his followers about the return of the Novena. Sometimes I heard vehicles in the yard, and the sound of voices, and whenever this happened I was worried that the door would swing open and the man in the suit would be standing there, declaring that I was unworthy. But no one came inside – not then, not until later. By the fourth day I had recovered much of my energy, and I suppose I could have escaped from the farm, if I hadn't been so worried about the dogs and if I could have imagined somewhere else to go. The rectory and the abbey were certainly out of the question. I had no money and, really, no friends; no one who would accept me for myself without labelling me either a heretic or a saint. Strangely, I felt safer in Lazarus's house than anywhere I could think of.

During that week when he brought me back to life, I began to come to terms with something. It was not a conversion or a dramatic revelation. Only a gradual acceptance that Lazarus was in earnest. What I had suspected at the Novena was true: he *had* changed. He really believed – in God, in me, in the possibility of salvation. He possessed the kind of unshaking conviction that I had always wanted.

I'll admit I envied him, though I knew his beliefs were nothing more than ridiculous fancies. I wished I could be so certain about anything, even something that was wrong. But I was afflicted with self-consciousness and intelligence and good judgment. I couldn't banish my doubt. It was, in a way, all I had left.

On my fifth day in his house we had a kind of confrontation, though it was nothing like the one I had planned for him at the Novena. I didn't *want* to confront him anymore, nor did I want to hear his theories on the nature of belief, but he provoked me to it. I had been sitting up in bed most of the afternoon, playing solitaire with a castaway deck of cards, while in the kitchen Lazarus read aloud from his pilfered Bible. I suspected he wasn't capable of reading silently, but perhaps he was simply practising for the next session of the Novena. I suffered through his diligent, plodding recitations for several hours, trying to ignore the all-familiar words and the strangely authoritative voice that was repeating them. Perhaps he saw it as some kind of marathon, like my Grandmother with her beads. It seemed that he was never going to stop. He had read the entire gospel of Luke and was starting in on the first chapter of John when I padded into the kitchen to watch him. He sat at the table, peering into the book before him and declaiming tirelessly, his left hand raised heavenward in a gesture of proclamation and his right hand tracing the words as he read them. The dogs were slumped in a canine heap beside the vibrating refrigerator, staring dreamily at me. They had become accustomed to his readings and no longer paid them much attention. Lazarus was so absorbed in his task that he continued reading for a couple more sentences before he realized I was there.

"'What has come into being in him was life, and the life was the light of all people. The light shines in the darkness, and the darkness did not overcome it.'"

He sensed my presence then, and lifted his shaggy head from the Bible to regard me with red-eyed piety. His greying, unkempt beard gave him a Santa Claus quality that was at odds with his bardic aspirations. I hadn't bathed in six days, and I was wearing my makeshift pyjamas: a sweat-stained undershirt and an impossibly wrinkled pair of black dress pants. I must have looked like a lunatic fresh off the ward.

"You're not just doing this to impress me," I said. "Are you? You really believe in it."

"Yes," he said without hesitation. "Of course I do."

"And you think I was responsible. For all this. Your second life."

He nodded, still keeping his place in the Bible with the stubby index finger of his right hand. "You and my wife. You were instruments of the Lord."

"But how can you believe such a thing when you know damn well that *I* don't believe it. And neither does your wife. *We were there.*"

"I was there too," he said. "And I know. You must have heard me describe it when I talked at the Novena. That's exactly what happened. I pray to God you'll believe me some day."

"But I won't," I replied. "So why do you keep trying to involve me? Why bring me here, why use my name in your prayers, why tell everyone I'm a great holy man, when I'm not?"

He looked away, back to the Bible and his grubby hand resting upon it, as if he could absorb holiness through his palm. "What do you think happened then, that night?"

"Nothing," I said. "I don't know. Not what you think."

We were both quiet for a while, as I tried to formulate a more satisfying answer to the question that had tormented me for weeks. But I couldn't come up with anything believable. The dogs snuffled and whined to each other, and the fridge hummed. Finally Lazarus shifted in his chair and spoke again.

"You're free to go whenever you want," he said. "I only helped because I saw you were in need."

"If you knew the truth about me you wouldn't have bothered. I've done you no favours. I was the one who encouraged Guadeloupe to leave you."

He only shrugged. "I made a poor husband."

"Yes," I said. "But I made a poor priest."

For the first time, I looked straight into his grey puzzled eyes. "I wanted her to come to me," I said.

He didn't respond, but I could see that he was shaken. He dropped his head more fully so I couldn't see his eyes. The edge of his beard and the wispy tufts of his greying sideburns were all I could see of his face. He seemed to be holding his breath, as if waiting for the onslaught to finish. I felt a kind of sympathy for him, despite the trials he had put me through. But I also knew that I couldn't stop there. I had to destroy the rest of his foolish notions.

"That's the kind of man I am," I said. "No hero, no spiritual leader, no healer. I don't even have any faith. And the moment when it happened, when I lost it – or when I realized it had never been there at all – was when I touched your face. Here in this bloody room. It wasn't a conversion, a resurrection. It was the moment when doubt gained a foothold in my soul."

Both of his hands were resting on the Bible now, his fingers interlaced. He clenched and unclenched them rhythmically, a habit he must have learned from watching Guadeloupe. He didn't respond for a long time. I thought he was either praying for strength or thinking about raising those fists against me.

"What do you say to that?" I asked.

He finally looked up into my eyes. "I say that the Lord forgives you, Father."

I realized then that I had confessed to him. To him, of all people! I had craved an audience for my anguish for so long, but not this. Nausea percolated in my throat.

"I don't need your absolutions," I said.

I almost walked past him out the front door and into the dangerous world, but still there was nowhere for me to go. So I fled back into the bedroom and flung myself onto the bed. After a few minutes I heard the screen door opening and the dogs crowding out behind Lazarus, but I made no attempt to escape. I stayed there, curled in the sweaty blankets, waiting for the dark shape to make its inevitable reappearance.

Lazarus didn't read the Bible in the house any more after that, though he took it with him whenever he went outside. He was gone for much of each day, mending fences and patching up the access road and generally preparing for the resumption of the Novena. Whenever he came back in, he seemed surprised to find me still there. I tried not to think about what I would do next. All of my options seemed equally impossible, so there was nothing to do but postpone my decision.

By the sixth day I had regained enough energy that I was able to prepare lunch and dinner when Lazarus was away. It gave me something to keep my mind off the absurdity of my situation. I refused to go outside to the garden, for fear of encountering a stray Novena fanatic, but Lazarus brought in fresh vegetables every morning, and he went to town once for supplies. If he had made any money on the Novena, he certainly hadn't started spending it yet. The groceries were as basic as possible: bacon, lard, flour, canned milk, instant coffee, forty-pound bags of generic dried dog food. The only luxury he permitted himself was a huge bag of chocolate macaroons, which were the dessert for every meal, breakfast included. We ate together at the kitchen table, talking only about subjects that wouldn't lead us into problems: the weather, the rapacity of bankers, the plague of tent caterpillars that threatened to denude every tree in his yard. He didn't say whether he liked the food or not, but he always ate everything on his plate.

When I wasn't cooking, I spent most of my time peering out the windows, trying to keep myself hidden behind the orange floral-print curtains that Guadeloupe must have made. I wanted to watch the comings and goings of Lazarus and his increasing band of helpers, but I also wanted to remain invisible myself. Sometimes trucks or delapidated vans came into the yard, and I feared that the Novena shanty town might appear again overnight. But the visitors always left before suppertime. They were only preparing for the Novena. They dragged old bird cages off into the bush, and a couple of them repainted Lazarus's precious truck, smearing a gallon of black housepaint on it with oversized brushes. One afternoon they dug two holes beside the old barn and then constructed makeshift outhouses from second-hand lumber. Sometimes they just stood together out in the yard, talking and occasionally nodding in the direction of the house. They knew I was there, but none of them ever came to the door. I wondered if they still believed in me, after what they had seen me do.

It was the tenth day of my stay when I received a visitor of my own. I was standing at the kitchen table, peeling carrots into a slop pail, when I noticed a flash of movement outside the window. Somehow I knew this was not one of the usual Novena vehicles. I dropped everything, the carrot and the peeler, and I ran to the half-closed curtains. But such confirmation was hardly necessary. Sure enough, when I closed the curtains more carefully and peered out from between them, I saw the K-car, and the shape of Father Remy's bespectacled bald head behind the wheel. He came to a halt beside a barren rectangle in the grass where one of the bird cages had been. He wrestled with the column shifter for a moment and then reluctantly climbed out, holding a small paper bag in his left hand.

I prayed that Lazarus and the dogs would frighten him away, but I knew they had gone out to the hayfield after lunch and they probably weren't close enough to hear the car. Maybe I should have cried out to them for help, or at least I should have hidden under the bedclothes, or scrambled into the closet behind Guadeloupe's old dresses. But I did nothing at all. I had known somewhere in my mind that this was going to happen, and now that it was upon me it had the inevitability of a dream. I stood there with the curtains clutched in my fists while he strode up to the front of the house and knocked tentatively at the screen door. I could see him through the glass, leaning forward with his hands cupped beside his eye-glasses to block out the glare. Apparently he still couldn't see me. He reached down to the handle and eased the door open, calling out "Alloooo?" He stopped in his tracks when he finally saw me, and his face flushed red, even up past his forehead into the polished skin of his scalp. I thought for a moment that his heart was failing him, but then he began to breathe, and he stepped into the room and offered me his hand, as if greeting a parishioner at the back of the church. I reached toward him automatically and he clasped my hand, gently, squinting down at me through his bifocals with a pinched expression of concern. I had hardly ever shaken his hand since the first time we'd met, eleven years earlier. His fingers were smooth and bony and utterly dry.

"My God, my God," he said. "I heard the stories but I didn't believe them. We were so worried, you know, everyone at the church and in the diocese. 'What has become of our Father Silvan?' they ask me, and I tell them I think he's gone out to find himself, to encounter with his faith. Others tell me you are here in this place, and I say, 'Why would he go there?' But sometimes I should listen more, I must learn to listen when people tell me things. Even when I don't understand."

Anyone would have thought he was in earnest. Maybe he was. It was hard to believe that this befuddled old scarecrow had excited so much hatred in me only a few days earlier. Probably it was the same for him: the longer I was gone, the more he could believe that he really missed me. I pulled my hand away from him and bent down to pick up the half-peeled carrot and the peeler, which were near his feet.

"Understanding is not always possible, Father," I said as I stood up. I placed the carrot and the peeler on the table beside the slop pail. "But we have to act on whatever evidence we have."

He considered this for a while, trying to decide what I might be referring to. He was wearing his full priestly regalia – all black except the white collar. I realized that I too was wearing my black shirt. I had stopped associating it with priestliness.

"Yes," he said. "But when we act we should have the benefit of advice. Spiritual guidance and the advice of friends. That's why I came here, to give you that benefit, to allow you a chance to see things from another perspective. We all need that sometime."

"What does the Bishop say?" I asked. "He was the one who sent you here. You would never have come on your own."

He looked disappointed at this, and a hint of anger smouldered briefly behind his bifocals.

"You know the consequences, I think. If you don't come back…."

"But if I do? I think the consequences wouldn't be much different. I'd be sent as far away as possible. A prison chaplaincy in the Yukon maybe."

He smiled, with his mouth only, and produced an exaggerated shrug. "You know I don't make these decisions. But I came here on my own, to offer you my friendship, and to help you decide what is best for the Church and for your soul."

"I'm doing what I can here, Father," I said. "I don't need any further help. Tell the Bishop that I'm examining my conscience, and I'll come back when I can."

He seemed almost relieved, as if he had expected this but had felt obligated to pursue a conciliatory approach.

"You will not take advice?"

"No."

"No. Then I shouldn't stay," he said. He turned toward the door without saying goodbye, but when he reached it he looked back at me with half a smile on his face, as if we were casual acquaintances and he was about to tell a joke.

"I forgot I had some other news. The girl, you know, she's gone. She moved away. But before she left she brought this to me."

He held the paper bag toward me, and I took it and pulled out a clump of white tissue paper. It was almost weightless. I began carefully unravelling the layers.

"I guess it hit the kitchen window there," he said, "where she was staying, and when she come up to the rectory she was holding it so delicate, with both hands cupped together, like she thought it might still be alive. She was crying. She said for me to fix it up and give it to you."

It was a tiny bird, a sparrow. Stuffed, and mounted on a disc of cross-cut wood. Its back was mottled brown and white, its poll grey, and across its breast there was a crescent of black feathers, like a sash or a breastplate. I trembled as I held it. The eyes had been replaced with opaque glass beads, like the ones from my grandmother's rosary.

"I done the best I could," he said, "but it's so small, you know, and my fingers they don't obey so well anymore. The fine work gives me trouble."

It had the right shape, but it was utterly dead. No one would ever mistake it for the real thing. Its posture was wrong – it seemed to be listing to one side – and those eyes were so blank it was difficult to look at them. I imagined the rolls of string or the pieces of styrofoam he had stuffed into the cavity. I remembered the birds that came every spring to make their nests in the prairie maples beside the rectory. So aflutter, so quirky with unending movement. Entirely different from this lifeless little thing in my hands.

"Anyway," he was saying, "she never said why to do this, but I done it as a favour to her. And to you. I wanted you to have one for yourself."

"Thank you, Father," I said. "Goodbye."

"Yes. I'll pray for you."

"Goodbye."

He left then, without a word of advice – which must have been a first for him. I heard the к-car starting, and then the rattle of its valves as it retreated down the laneway. I continued staring at the inanimate bird, wondering what Guadeloupe might have meant, and even considering the possibility that she hadn't done it at all, that Father Remy had invented the whole story for some perverse reason of his own.

The sound of the κ-car had barely faded when Lazarus appeared at the door. He hovered outside for a moment and then he pushed his way in, holding the door open as the dogs filed in behind him. I knew he had been watching us from a distance. He studied me with urgent concern, his eyes moving from my face to the preposterous bird, his mouth half open like it had been when I'd found him on the kitchen table.

"You don't have to go," he said.

"For you," I answered, and I placed the sparrow in his unsuspecting hands.

DAY EIGHTY
HOUSE OF THE RESURRECTION

hree days after Father Remy's visit, the Novena began again. Lazarus suggested it, and I saw no reason for further delay. Not that I had experienced a change of heart, or received any thunderous revelations. I didn't learn to believe by watching him. He didn't save my soul. But I began to play along with him because it was easier than constantly asserting my doubt. Besides, I saw that I had power over him, and over others, because they believed in me. I remembered the roar of the crowd that had held the two of us aloft. I had felt a kind of mastery over Lazarus since his wedding day, when I'd seen him standing at the altar of the church, shifting his feet and staring with childlike gloom at the twenty-foot crucifix on the wall behind me, as if even then he had a premonition of what he would become. Now, as I acquiesced to his fervid certainty, I understood that I would become his mentor, his spiritual advisor. Despite my own scepticism, I was to be the fountain of his faith.

I tested his sincerity by asking him to fire Mr. Bernier, the man in the suit who had elected himself as the Novena's stage manager. I threatened to leave unless this man was dismissed. Lazarus got rid of him that very day without a word of complaint. He never told me how it was done, he simply obeyed. After that, he began to consult me on every aspect of the Novena, asking what Bible readings would be appropriate for each day, what prayers were most propitious, how he should take collection. I composed my own ministry there in the musty kitchen, with old moonshine bottles still rolling around on the floor as reminders of Lazarus's old life. I created a dogma and a creed and a ritual. I planned every moment of the Novena, and Lazarus carried it out.

My final test of his loyalty was to ask for the money. Without hesitation, he jogged out into the bush behind the granaries and returned with a gunny sack full of change and bills, which he placed carefully on the edge of the bed.

"I kept it hidden so Mr. Bernier couldn't get at it," he said, "but now we'll do what you want." And we did. I left him in charge of hiding the offerings, since I knew by then I could trust him.

For the first few days after the Novena resumed, I watched from the house, moving from window to window, keeping my face hidden from the crowd. I heard people in the congregation marvelling about my miraculous appearance at the previous Novena, and recalling with wonder my baptism of their leader. It didn't matter that I had really tried to kill him. Whatever they might have thought about it at the time, Lazarus had talked them into seeing it another way. Once, they had declared me unworthy, but now they saw my actions as sacramental, nearly miraculous. Such is the perversity of belief.

Finally I gave in to Lazarus's pleading and agreed to take part in the Novena. I stood in the truck box with him and said whatever I thought they wanted to hear. At first I wasn't good at it: I lacked the prophetic certitude that Lazarus had perfected. But I learned that it didn't matter. The people still listened in awe. I could have given readings from the telephone book and they would have regarded every word as holy revelation. They believed in me as fervently as Lazarus did.

They still do. The two of us go out every day at noon, and the crowds continue to grow. The people throw themselves on the ground near the truck, and I tell them they are forgiven for their sins. Sick people come too, and the lame and the blind, and we prop them up on the edge of the tailgate, and I push them off into the waiting crowd. And sometimes they are healed! It happens, I don't know how. Because they want it to. I have healed dozens of them already. We have begun a collection of crutches.

Somehow this is related to the dark shape of doubt that inhabits me still. My one remaining superstition is that these miracles can only happen as long as I don't believe. If I began to have faith in the dark shape, to believe in my powers, they would fail. As long as I know I am acting, and there is no power inside me, the people will do the believing. Their conviction is what cures them.

It might be said that I have done more good here, in the last thirty-seven days, than I did in two decades of priesthood. But I don't know. It is a frightening thing to be at the centre of that pulsing throng of charismatics every day, knowing that I am the alpha and omega of their every frantic thought, that I inform their breath and their heartbeats – and that all of it is a lie. Knowing that I am a charlatan, a faker, a liar, an unbeliever at the centre of a new and living faith: it makes me the emptiest creature in the world. Sometimes when I'm standing there in the truck box with Lazarus slavering at my side, I want to die or disappear, or simply to tell the awestruck congregation that none of it is true, that Lazarus was never dead and I have not performed a miracle. But their belief will not allow this. I am as much a slave to it as they are. I had thought I would be the master, but instead I've become the acolyte, the necessary cipher, the puppet of their delusions.

The end of the Novena comes tomorrow. We will re-enact the resurrection then, at the kitchen table. I will come in and place my hands on Lazarus's head, and then he will arise. And in the infallible eyes of the people, it will become another miracle. The next day Lazarus and I will pack up our belongings and our dogs, and we will move on to another place, where there are more people who need us. This is a crusade, a never-ending task. So much credulity, so little time.

I have learned that everyone wants to believe. It is an innate need, inexplicable and eternal, like our requirement for food or for sexual gratification. This is why, despite my frail-ties, I am indispensable. My curse can become a blessing – not for me, but for the legions of believers. They will keep coming to me, and their needs will keep pouring into the chasm of my disbelief. And they will never fill it up.

ABOUT THE AUTHOR

Warren Cariou was one of three featured authors in *Coming Attractions '95*, and has had short stories appear in *Stag Line: Stories by Men*, and *Due West*, both published by Coteau Books. As well, his fiction was awarded a CBC Literary Competition Prize in 1991. This is his first solo book publication.

Warren Cariou grew up on a farm near Meadow Lake, Saskatchewan. He has worked as a construction labourer, a technical writer, and a political aide. He has a Ph.D from the University of Toronto, and is currently a lecturer at the University of British Columbia.

ACKNOWLEDGMENTS

I want to express my gratitude to the Saskatchewan Arts Board for its support during the writing of this book. Thanks also to the Banff Centre and the Saskatchewan Artists/Writers Colonies for providing inspiration and comradeship. On a personal level, I owe a great deal to Sandra Birdsell, Alistair MacLeod, Dave Margoshes, and my editor David Carpenter for their encouragement, criticism, and good humour. Thanks, finally, to Alison Calder, who has helped in countless ways.

– W. Cariou